MW01531327

CHECK CANOPY

JACK WELSH

outskirts
press

Check Canopy
All Rights Reserved.
Copyright © 2017 Jack Welsh
v6.0 r1.0

This is a work of fiction. The events and characters described herein are imaginary and are not intended to refer to specific places or living persons. The opinions expressed in this manuscript are solely the opinions of the author and do not represent the opinions or thoughts of the publisher. The author has represented and warranted full ownership and/or legal right to publish all the materials in this book.

This book may not be reproduced, transmitted, or stored in whole or in part by any means, including graphic, electronic, or mechanical without the express written consent of the publisher except in the case of brief quotations embodied in critical articles and reviews.

Outskirts Press, Inc.
http://www.outskirtspress.com

Paperback ISBN: 978-1-4787-8982-6

Cover & Interior Images © 2017 by John Welsh. All rights reserved - used with permission.

Outskirts Press and the "OP" logo are trademarks belonging to Outskirts Press, Inc.

PRINTED IN THE UNITED STATES OF AMERICA

An Army Colonel fights a losing battle with kidney disease while reflecting on his life. He grew up in a strict Catholic family, played intercollegiate club football at a small college and spent a year working as a third helper in an open hearth steel mill in Homestead, Pennsylvania. He then enlisted in the Army and spent a thirty-five year career in the military and government, starting as a Private First Class in an infantry battalion in Germany and ending with command of an airborne battalion at Fort Bragg with a follow-on assignment as a Colonel on the Joint Staff in the Pentagon.

The title of the book refers to one of the procedures a paratrooper must perform after exiting the aircraft. There are many checks and procedures that need to be performed prior to exiting the aircraft and others required during descent and landing. The only check that truly reassures the paratrooper that he will survive the jump is when the trooper counts to four after the exit, feels an opening shock and looks up and sees a billowing canopy fully opened. Every now and then in life it is important to check your canopy, making sure that no matter what else is happening, you can have a safe landing.

This is a work of fiction. While items are based on experience, names are pseudonyms and circumstances have been modified. Any similarity to any person living or dead is merely coincidental. The views expressed here are those of the authors alone.

Table of Contents

Quote:

"What manner of men are these who wear the maroon beret. They are firstly volunteers and are toughened by hard physical training. As a result, they have that infectious optimism and that offensive eagerness which comes from physical wellbeing. They have "jumped" from the air and by so doing have conquered fear. Their duty lies in the van of battle; they are proud of this honor and have never failed in any task. They have the highest standards in all things whether it be skill in battle or smartness in the execution of all peacetime duties. They have shown themselves to be tenacious and determined in the defense as they are courageous in the offense. They are in fact soldiers apart – every trooper an emperor. Of all the factors which make for success in battle this spirit of the warrior is the most decisive. That spirit can be found in full measure in the men who wear the maroon beret".

Field Marshall The Viscount Montgomery of Alamein.

About the Author

The author graduated from college in 1974 with a degree in English. He was a member of the intercollegiate club football team. After graduation, he spent one year working at United States Steel Homestead Works. He then enlisted in the Army as a private first class and spent 28 years and nine months in the military, culminating in assignment as a battalion commander of an airborne (paratrooper) battalion at Fort Bragg, North Carolina and a follow on assignment at the Joint Staff in the Pentagon. He retired as a Colonel on January 1, 2004. After retirement he continued to work in the Pentagon, first as a contractor and subsequently as a government civilian employee. In March 2009, he was diagnosed with end state kidney failure requiring dialysis for the rest of his life or a transplant. This book was written for 2 reasons:

1. To encourage people to take care of themselves. Watch your diet, exercise, invest in a blood pressure cuff and take your blood pressure every day at the same time and do what your doctor tells you. If you have a stressful job, find an outlet to relax. Do not be in denial.

2. If you do have kidney failure, you can still have a full life. The author's kidneys failed 9 years ago. Dialysis is a medical marvel and a transplant is a miracle. In the nine years since diagnosis, the author was able to work; watch his two children complete graduate school

and begin professional careers and he walked his daughter down the aisle.

A portion of the proceeds from this book will be donated to the National Kidney Foundation and the book is dedicated to his sister, Nancy Winship, who provided the ultimate selfless act of donating a kidney (which she named Sidney after the Pittsburgh Penguins star center).

Chapter 1
Failure

Frank was lying on a gurney in a small room barely large enough for the gurney, the anesthesiologist and the nurse. It was probably best that he could not see what was in store for him. Better that he did not see the doctor, technicians and machines that awaited him on the other side of the door. The anesthesiologist opened a valve to the needle lodged in his arm and told Frank to start counting backwards from 100. He only got to 98.

On March 29, 2010, Frank was diagnosed with end state renal (kidney) failure and was placed on dialysis. This involved being connected to a dialysis machine for four hours per dialysis session, three times per week. Frank continued to work in the Pentagon. His co-workers and bosses were amenable to him leaving work at 1530 three days per week to arrive for the session by 1600. This required careful planning to ensure he did not get hung up in D.C. traffic. Often, during good weather, he would drive a motorcycle, and that gave him access to the HOV lane. Being on dialysis precluded him from traveling to conduct site visits or attend conferences for work, although that was not a huge problem since his organization was short or out of travel funds for most of the year and emphasized use of video and teleconferences. He did take one trip to Bonn, Germany for work. One of his employees told him that he was too sick to travel.

This was on a Sunday for a NATO conference on in transit visibility that was to start on Tuesday. Frank called his boss and told her that he could attend. Frank rarely missed a dialysis session but he noticed other patients routinely missed, much to the chagrin of the staff at the clinic. Frank decided that he could take a dialysis session on Monday morning and leave for Germany that afternoon. He would arrive in Frankfurt on Tuesday morning and take a bullet train to Bonn and get there around 1000 in the morning. He would definitely miss a Wednesday dialysis session but hoped to either make the Friday afternoon session or ask for a special session on Saturday. His nurse at the clinic was furious, but Frank left on Monday afternoon. It was a great conference. A joke about NATO was that they would hold a weeklong conference just to set the agenda for the following conference and that decisions were almost never made. This was not the case. The conference was attended by computer experts and once the preliminaries were over, they got down to work. They spent long days developing processes and supporting systems, proving that computer experts were obsessed with their profession s regardless of nationality or organization. There were several cultural events included in the agenda. Bonn was located in the wine region of Germany and the conference attendees took a tour of a winery then went to a restaurant that overlooked the Rhine River for a great six course meal. Frank had served in Germany for three tours (11 years), but mostly in Bavaria. Being in the wine region was a totally different experience. Even the train ride from the Frankfurt Flughafen to Bonn was incredible. The train travelled directly along the Rhine river. It was like taking a Rhine River cruise at 70 miles per hour, passing all the castles and vineyards that line the river. He did return in time to take a Saturday session and did not appear to have any health issues resulting from missing the session. Also while he was there he was given a lanyard as part of a Swag Bag to commemorate the visit. Frank had a Breckenridge ski resort lanyard that he had been using for years but under the weight of more than 8 badges (most were required for his job at the Pentagon but some were souvenirs from trips to Kuwait and Iraq) that lanyard broke while he was on the trip. The lanyard attendees were given said Bonn: Beethoven Stadt. Frank used that during the conference with the intention of replacing it when he got back to the states. When he returned he had an appointment at Walter Reed and he got on the elevator with a nice looking young lady. Frank was surprised when she asked him if he was a Beethoven fan. Frank normally did not have nice looking young women talk to him on elevators and he was somewhat confused until he remembered that he was wearing the lanyard. He said he was a big Beethoven fan. That incident convinced him to keep the Beethoven lanyard (a little culture was never a bad thing) and it reminded him of a great trip.

He was able to take two short vacations to Florida. This necessitated a local dialysis session, but was really not an issue as the local dialysis office made arrangements with a dialysis clinic in Florida. This required an advance notice but the staff at the local clinic really hustled to make sure that he was able to go to Florida. It is probably not known to most people, but there are dialysis clinics on virtually every street corner and shopping center in America. Frank has always intended to write a novel but never found the time to actually sit down and start writing. There was always something to do, even if it was just to go outside because it was a nice day. He started several times and never really got past the first page. Dialysis did provide him with time. Dialysis required the patient to be hooked up to a machine for four hours three times a week. He would arrive from work tired and after the pencil thick needle was inserted into his arm (fortunately most of the technicians could get a vein on the first try, due in part to the fistula in his left arm) and the technicians would then adjust the machine. There were 13 chairs and they were all full. Most were minorities. The disease seems to hit African Americans hard. Frank was one of the few who was still able to work. Some were in very bad shape with other complications or even amputations due to diabetes. Everyone weighed in prior to the treatment and typically the technician would set up the machine to remove 8 lbs. of fluid. If they had to remove more, that would result in cramps near the end of the session. The techs were great at dealing with leg cramps. One of his favorite technicians was a black female who had served in the Army. She was sturdy enough to allow Frank to place his foot on her thigh and then bend his toes back when he had a cramp. That usually relieved the pain. Often though, he would get a cramp in his stomach and there was nothing to do but take the pain. If he was still hooked up, the technician could give him back some fluid and that would relieve the pain, but until that stomach cramp went away, it was extremely painful.

When Frank road his motorcycle, he would often cramp up on the ride home. This was not good on a motorcycle as it was not possible to straighten out fingers or legs while riding down the road. Many times he had to pull over and wait, but the trip from the dialysis center to his house was only about 5 miles.

The dialysis process lasted 4 hours (although he sometimes talked his way into 3 and one half hours). Frank would typically fall asleep for the first half hour. When he woke up he would work for about one hour using either his blackberry or a laptop. He then would work on his novel. He did a rough outline but mostly he wrote a phrase or name that would remind him of something that he would try to fit into the novel. Then he just began writing. Frank was a good typist but being on dialysis forced him to type with his right hand only as his left was hooked up to the machine and could not move. He started writing and was amazed at how much he could accomplish with a dedicated hour and one half. At first the novel took a few different directions but Frank finally settled on a plot and characters. It really just flowed from there.

Dialysis was the worst experience of Frank's life but this novel would not have been written if not for the dedicated time that was forced upon him.

Frank continued to work long hours and travel after he retired but there was considerably less pressure. After retirement, Frank worked for two years on the Joint Staff doing essentially the same planning job he had been doing during active duty as a contractor. During this time, he took two trips to Afghanistan and Iraq as part of high level assessment teams led by three star generals. Frank had not been to Iraq or Afghanistan while on active duty but went there often as a civilian. At the 2 year, point he transitioned from being a contractor working on site at the Pentagon to being a government employee. He liked to say he held out for less pay and fewer benefits as contractor work in D.C was plentiful with 2 wars going on. As a government employee, Frank's travel ratcheted up.

It wasn't until about thirty days prior to total failure that Frank could tell that he was indeed being slowly poisoned by his kidney malfunction. This occurred four years after he retired.

Chapter 2

The Pentagon

Frank told his coworkers that he had to leave early to catch his son's football game. "If the front office calls, tell them I am in the Pentagon Officer's Athletic Club (POAC)". Now that the Afghanistan war was essentially over, it was assumed that the military would begin enforcing weight standards when screening officers for promotion. Time spent at the POAC was rarely questioned. Frank's son had gone out for freshman football at Robinson High. This was somewhat of a rite of passage for young boys. He had never played on a football team. Having spent seven of his thirteen years in Germany, he had always played soccer and he was very good at it. He was both quick and fast. He was certainly on the thin side, but he assumed he could play defensive back due to his speed. On the first day of practice, he gained the attention of the coach by winning all twelve 60 yard wind sprints The head coach said that he didn't know if that kid could play football, but he was going to be the safety on the kickoff team He also impressed the defensive back coach when running drills though cones. From his soccer playing days, he was good at changing direction quickly and keeping his head up. Robinson, like most high schools in Northern Virginia, has a no cut policy for football. This typically results in a freshman football team of seventy-five kids. While there are a few superstars, the emphasis for the freshman team is on discipline and learning Robinson's offensive and defensive schemes. They ran simple formations that required every man to do precisely what was required. This system had created a powerhouse and the freshmen were eager to take their place in this dynasty. The first game was against Lake Braddock, a rival school less than two miles away in the densely populated suburbs of Northern Virginia. Robinson quickly scored two touchdowns and Frank's son was sent in to give the quarterback/safety a breather. On the first play he was in, the Lake Braddock quarterback, under heavy pressure, threw a wounded duck pass that landed about 10 feet in front of Frank's son. The next play, he threw a perfect spiral right to his son, who intercepted it. He hesitated for a second, stiff-armed the receiver who had fallen to the ground in front of him, and then began heading for the sideline. Frank was his typical nervous self at sporting events involving his kids. He was far too hyper to sit in the stands and was nervously pacing the sidelines down by the track. His wife sat with a few other wives in the bleachers with the video camera. Frank was thrilled as he watched his son head for the sideline. At about the 50 yard line, virtually all 21 other players on the field converged. All assumed he would be knocked out of bounds. His son disappeared in a mass of jerseys. Then there was a rumbling from the fans on the Lake Braddock side who were closest to the action, then a loud cheer erupted from the visiting Robinson fans. Frank could not see because he was at ground level. His son somehow emerged from the mass and was now sprinting down the sideline for the end zone. The quarterback made one last attempt to tackle him but misjudged the angle. He crossed the goal line and handed the ball to the official like he had done this hundreds of times before. Then he stood there and was mobbed by his teammates and coaches. At that point, everyone on the team realized that the Robinson dynasty in football was safe for at least another 4 years if kids who had never played before could enter a game, intercept a pass and run it back for a touchdown. When Frank asked his son how he managed to get through all of the opposing players near the sidelines, he said that his own players were throwing vicious blocks and created a huge gap for him to pass through. No one laid a hand on him.

Frank's kids had a more normal life than most Army kids, but they did have the typical moves. Both had gone to Department of Defense Schools in Germany and both had spent a few years going to school in Fayetteville, North Carolina. The Fayetteville experience was quite unique. The soccer field at Fort Bragg was the emergency landing site for helicopters in distress. All players had to be familiar with emergency evacuation procedures in the event that a helicopter had to use the field to land.

Frank's daughter was on the swim team at Fort Bragg, which also qualified her to swim as a varsity athlete for Pine Forest Senior High School. She lettered in swimming her first two years at the school and while she didn't think it was a big deal, the boys who played football and basketball were impressed that a freshman had earned a varsity letter. She enjoyed the attention. In the summer, she worked as a lifeguard, but could only be an assistant until she turned sixteen. She came home from her first day helping at one of the pools in the 82d Airborne area and she told Frank that she had met these cool guys with big muscles and tattoos. Frank went to the pool the next day and assembled all of the paratroopers who had been detailed for life guard duty and told them that his daughter was only 15 and she was off limits. They got the message and in fact Frank actually felt that these guys would do everything in their power to protect her.

Frank's daughter was also learning to drive that summer and Frank thought it would be a good idea to drive on Fort Bragg on the road that went past all the drop zones because there would be very little traffic. The road was not really all that well constructed and had sharp turns and a lot of blind crests on hills. As Frank and his daughter were cresting one of the hills, an Apache helicopter going almost 200 miles per hour and flying nap of the earth (about 20 feet above the ground) was cresting the hill coming toward Frank and his daughter. There is nothing in a driver's training manual that tells you what to when an Apache helicopter is filling up your entire windshield. They were so close they could see that the pilot had a mustache and he was probably only a little less shocked than the passengers in the car. They missed colliding by about 10 feet.

Frank's daughter was between 10th and 11th grade when the family moved from Fayetteville to Northern Virginia. His son was entering 7th grade. They arrived in Virginia and moved into a rental house on Wednesday and his daughter was already working as a lifeguard on Thursday. She had no problem making friends and adjusting. She could adjust to the move from a school district in Fayetteville to one of the best high schools in the country, even though she was a normal student getting B's and the occasional A in Fayetteville. She somehow got through chemistry and algebra (thanks to a programmable calculator) and she was able to adjust to the move. It was more difficult for his son, but he eventually made friends by participating in sports. He had no problem academically as he had always been a strong student.

Chapter 3

September 11

One week after his son's first football game the attack on the Pentagon and the World Trade Center took place. Incredibly, Frank was not in the Pentagon on that day. His father had died the week before and Frank was not sure when the funeral would take place. Frank was back from the funeral on Tuesday September 11 2001, but was still on leave when the plane crashed into the Pentagon. He did receive a few phone calls to include from his in laws in Germany asking if he was all right. He also received a call from two of his son's teammates from his soccer team who were of Jordanian descent. Frank had traveled with them to England for a soccer tournament. They were great kids from a nice family and Frank appreciated the call. He also received a call from the Pentagon telling him to report to work. He traveled to the Pentagon on deserted roads to find the Pentagon in flames. His badge got him through the extremely heightened security and he entered what was a smoke filled building. He reported to the Joint Logistics Operations Center that was in the National Military Command Center. That part of the building was over pressured and there was no smoke or evidence of what was taking place outside. Frank found the operations center relatively calm, but that was because no one really knew what to do. Military people liked to operate with plans and SOPs and synch matrices. They lived in a world of flexible deterrent options and gradual escalation. Since Frank was a paratrooper, he was more prepared than most for no notice operations. He began to assess what was going on. Clearly there was a close in battle right there at the Pentagon and it was obvious that troop movements would begin. In fact, one of the units that was under his command while he was at Fort Bragg, a detachment of a laundry and bath company, was requested, presumably to support the Special Forces. Frank assumed that special ops guys were already deploying there. This laundry and bath unit always supported the Special Forces and had developed a solid relationship with them. His soldiers loved deploying with the Green Berets and especially liked the Robin Sage exercises where the Green Beret candidates were dropped off in the North Caronia country side and expected to accomplish missions by building relationships with the locals. Frank could not have been prouder.

There was a lot of discussion about graves registration in the operations center Frank did not advocate deploying one of these companies because they would no doubt be needed to support the overseas deployments. As all in the Crisis Action Center were trying to figure out what to do, Frank suggested that a couple guys go outside and see what was happening. It was incredible that officers working in the nerve center of the nation's defense could actually walk outside to get the real story on what was happening. That certainly was never envisioned in any plan. Frank called a friend in the Army Operations Center and he said they were going to go out in about thirty minutes and he said he could take a few Joint Staff guys with them as long as they didn't bring any generals. Frank and a couple action officers linked up with the Army staff officers and went outside. They again got though the tight security and were able to walk right up to the site of the crash. The first thing they noticed was numerous federal agencies were already on site. The Pentagon is a federal building. A small city was beginning to form in the parking lot with fire trucks, cranes, generators and lights sets were already set up. The FBI was there in force with doctors, scientists and special agents. Also there was the Old Guard, the Washington D.C. ceremonial unit. While everyone in the building was wondering what to do and who to mobilize, the Old Guard immediately sprang into action. Being an infantry unit, they have always had the mission to defend Washington D.C. and their Command Sergeant Major was on the scene organizing the graves registration mission. They had already contracted for refrigeration units for use as a temporary morgue and were well into the process of identifying the deceased. It was good to know that things happened the way they were supposed to in the absence of orders. Frank went back in and was asked to brief the highest levels of the Defense Department Leadership in the morning. The brief was well received.

Frank worked nights for the next thirty days. It was great work because it wasn't typical staff work. Staff officers were actually moving units and equipment. The only drawback was that Frank's boss wanted them to hang around through the next morning in case something was required. He typically worked from 1700 to 1100 the next morning. Working in the morning also had the drawback of leaving the National Military Command Center and working in regular office areas which were filled with smoke and very uncomfortable. During the night, Frank could either take a quick catnap or go outside to get something to eat at Harris Teeters. Eventually organizations started setting up tents and trailers in the parking lot to feed the firemen, FBI agents and night shift workers. There was a huge contingent from a North Carolina Baptist Church that prepared great food. There was also an Outback Steakhouse trailer. Incredibly you could go out and get a steak. That was great for morale

Frank's boss asked him if he could do some work on with the Office of the Secretary of Defense to work with other countries to secure logistics and basing rights. It did involve meeting with high level OSD officials. Frank was invited to go on a trip to the Mideast with high ranking DoD officials and a few others as part of this program. Frank had to get a few Visas so he spent a day going to various embassies. The team traveled to several Mideast countries. On the last stop, since Frank was with an Undersecretary, the team had an office call with the country's Secretary of Defense. Of course his office was a palace. In fact, his office was like nothing Frank had ever seen. It was the size of a basketball court with 40 foot ceilings. Priceless tapestries hung from the ceiling to the floor. Everything was the best. Mahogany furniture. What wasn't in the office was any evidence that any work was ever done. No phone, no computer, no reference material, no in and out box. Perhaps that took place in another room. The talks with the defense secretary/prince moved quickly from business to pleasure. They agreed to provide the requested aid. He also mentioned that his country was of great assistance in the take down of Kandahar airfield. Frank was somewhat incredulous at hearing this as the airfield was seized by Rangers and Marines. The defense secretary said that his office provided maps and detailed plans. He then quickly changed the conversation to horses. They talked about horses until lunch. They then were treated to an extravagant lunch. Maine lobster, caviar, steak, fruits and vegetables, all from exotic locations. Frank had never seen such opulence and frankly it made him uncomfortable. Frank and a few of the other members of the team went back to the hotel and got ready for the next leg of the trip to Pakistan. The Undersecretary and his deputy stayed at the palace. They were to have dinner with a dignitary. When Frank and the rest of the team arrived at the airport, they were told that the Undersecretary and his deputy were delayed. That meant the plane (a commercial airliner) was delayed. He and his deputy arrived at the airport by helicopter about an hour after the plane should have departed. The entire team got on the plane, but most of the team was in first class. Frank and another Colonel were back in steerage. The plane was full except for the two seats that were left for the Colonels at opposite ends of the third class cabin. Both of the Colonels had huge carry-on bags and of course there was no longer any room in the overhead compartments. The stewardesses grabbed the bags and put them back where they were seated. Everyone on the plane was glaring at the two Americans, who were in civilian clothes, but it is not too difficult to pick out an American. Frank sat next to a woman in full Burka with a child. She immediately called for the stewardess and said she did not want to sit next to the infidel. The stewardess moved her and told the other Colonel he could sit next to Frank. To everyone on the plane it looked like Frank had the lady and her kid moved so the two Americans could sit together. Not only had they delayed the plane for over an hour but now they had kicked a local out of her seat. Incredibly there was free alcohol on the flight to Pakistan. There was nothing to do at that point but start drinking.

Upon arriving in Pakistan, the team stayed in a hotel near the Embassy that was still under construction. Almost nothing worked, and that, coupled with an almost exclusively male staff, really made for a miserable stay. They linked up with the ambassador and then went to see the Pakistani Secretary of Defense. This was a total contrast with the previous experiences. This SEC Def's office was clearly designed to be functional. Computers, television screens, phones and even a military radio were in the office. One of the things the U.S team was offering, was an offer made by Mid-East countries to conduct a training mission for the Pakistani Army. Frank had questioned the defense officials on this. Frank knew that the Pakistani Army was well trained and disciplined with most of their officers trained at Sandhurst and had implemented the British regimental system with its emphasis on pride, tradition and discipline. The Pakistanis had also been engaged in a semi hot war with India in the Kashmir region. Frank told the team that that for as long as he had been in the military, the Ordnance magazine would write an annual article on the effect of altitude on artillery performance, based on analysis of this conflict, which was typically waged at altitudes over 10,000 feet. There were very few militaries in the Middle East that were on a par with Pakistan. The comptroller said that the desk officer at OSD thought this offer of training by this country would be well received. When the Undersecretary made the offer, the Pakistan SEC DEF seemed confused. He asked why they would need the other country to train the Pakistani Army. The Undersecretary quickly said he agreed and that if anything, the Pakistani Army could be training the other country's Army. That was an ice breaker and the rest of the meeting went smoothly. After the meeting, they went back to the hotel. The deputy wanted to go downtown to the market so they all piled in a van and took off. She had to wear a head scarf. One of the action officers from CENTCOM got in the front seat and immediately began speaking Urdu to the driver. Frank had worked with him for two years and had no idea he could speak the local language. He was desperately trying to get stationed in Pakistan, but despite the fact that almost every military person had gone there kicking and screaming against their will for a two year tour (especially after dependents could no longer accompany the military) an officer who definitely wanted to go and not only spoke the language but was immersed in the culture, could not get assigned there. At any rate, he was valuable to the team because he got them all great deals on rugs. That night the team went out to a local restaurant with the Ambassador. As they were leaving, a group of Pakistanis arrived wearing the Salwar Kameez and Pakol headgear. There were about twenty men in the group, looking as if they had just come down from the mountains. Of the twenty men, at least ten were over six foot tall. They were all lean and had beards. Frank was beginning to understand why it was so hard to find Bin Laden. Half the people in the country looked just like him.

On the way home the team split up. Frank got on a plane that was scheduled to go from Islamabad to London, but a Pakistani Colonel got on the plane and the commercial plane was diverted to Lahore. This made Frank's arrival in London too late to make his connection. Frank linked up with a reporter from Fox news who was on the same plane and they went to see what the airline could do. Frank had stayed in a hotel near the airport before and was reasonably certain that they the airline would put them up in a nice place. The airline gave them a voucher for a hotel and the taxi ride, so Frank and the reporter got in the taxi together. They drove past all the airport hotels and traveled about 40 miles into a working class area and were dropped off in a converted apartment building that was now a hotel. Once the hotel desk clerk saw they had airline vouchers she placed them in rooms with no bathroom and no phone. They had a voucher for dinner, but had to order off the special Airlines menu. The Fox News reporter had an expense account and had had enough and he checked out. Frank, being on per diem, ended up staying.

Chapter 4
The Joint Staff

Working on the Joint Staff was a pretty good job prior to 9/11. Frank had fortunately spent one year at the Industrial College of the Armed Forces where he was able to get used to doing things on his own. While serving as a battalion commander, Frank essentially did nothing on his own. His driver would work the radio, read the map and even clean Frank's pistol. The clerical staff in the office did all his typing for him. When he entered battalion command, he was fairly proficient in computers and staff work. When he left two years later, he was virtually hopeless.

The year in ICAF got him used to using power point and writing staff studies again so he arrived on the Joint Staff ready to go. ICAF also emphasized life fitness. There was a sports program that fielded teams that would play against the National War College that was collocated with ICAF on Fort McNair. All sports were very competitive. ICAF even has a mascot and cheerleaders. It was all good practice for Jim Thorpe days that were hosted by the Army War College in Carlisle with the Naval War College, the Air Force War College and the two Joint Schools (National and ICAF) competing for the Chairman's trophy. Having men and women in the mid to late forties compete in various sports was risky and did result in some minor injuries, but provided a great outlet for stress and fostered team building and making connections that would pay off when senior leaders returned to their potions in the Defense Department or other branches of government (ICAF was about 1/3 civilians government employees from all branches of the government). Also included was a thorough physical that included a stress test. Frank was in peak condition from serving in an airborne unit and since he was over 45 he had to take annual physicals at Fort Bragg. The Fort Bragg physicals indicated a problem with Frank's kidneys which Frank just ignored. The main purpose of the physicals as far as Frank was concerned was to get the date of the physical annotated in his official record and that the height and weight on the physical matched the height and weight on his annual efficiency reports. ICAF was the first time the physical included a stress test which involved running on a treadmill while hooked up to sensors. . At the end of the test the Doctor said Frank's test was positive. Frank said Hooah and thought to himself of course it was, he was in great shape. The Doctor said I don't think you understand. Positive is not good. He was scheduled for an MRI and that began periodic checks at Walter Reed for heart disease as well as kidney failure.

Frank was in the information management concentration during the second semester. Although he was not a technical person, Frank was convinced that there had to be a way to pass large volumes of technical data over the internet.

While commanding a battalion at Fort Bragg, Frank partnered with a signal battalion. The battalion commander was a TAC officer when Frank had gone to Officer Candidate School and while they were adversaries during OCS, they became great friends at Fort Bragg. The two battalion commanders were committed to sending routine supply transactions to sources of supply. Although they made it work, it required large amounts of equipment and personnel. He wanted to know if industry was passing data as a matter of routine. The study group took a trip to Silicon Valley and met with several cutting edge industries. At one high tech firm a young guy was sent in to brief the students. He was wearing jeans and a T shirt and a beret. He was on the team that developed java. Frank realized that this would probably never happen in the Defense Department. The system of promotions and responsibility was so rigid that it would not enable talented young people, especially those that did not conform to the established norm, to excel and contribute by questioning current practices. In any event, the young guy was talking to the group and about mid-way through he stopped. The team was in civilian clothes but it finally dawned on him that he was speaking to military personnel. He said he hadn't ever given the military much thought but he could really help us. He explained some things that he could do by making slight changes to commercial applications. He then quickly described designs of robots to disarm bombs, remote control planes to take video or even drop bombs, small devices that could see over the next ridge or around the next corner. Frank came away thing there must be a way to attract people like him to the Defense Department and move away from a five year acquisition cycle. The team (about 13 people) also took a trip to the Far East. The team went to Singapore and Japan, and Frank did significantly improve his knowledge of what was technically feasible. Since most of the team aside from Frank were technology experts by trade, they took advantage of the inexpensive software in Singapore. One guy had a duffle bag full of software and Frank joked that he would be like the guy in Midnight Express with is heart pounding as he passed through customs.

After graduation Frank was assigned to the Joint Staff at the Pentagon. On the Joint Staff, everyone was on their own. There were some secretaries but they were pooled and they certainly didn't work for action officers. Frank was assigned to work in plans and exercises and he had three contractors working for him. They were great employees who would rather die than let Frank or the organization down. Serving on the Joint Staff was a prerequisite for making flag officer, so the military guys came and went fairly rapidly, usually staying the bare minimum of 24 months then going back to their original service (Army, Navy, Air Force, Marines) to get command and or promotion. The civilians and contractors on the Joint staff provided continuity. When Frank arrived, Kosovo was just winding down. That was a big event for the J4 because that war was essentially about supporting refugees and precision ammunition, both of which were J4 functions. As that wound down, the next big thing was Y2K. Frank never really understood the problem, but the J7 was tasked to assemble a team to go PACOM to assess plans for Y2K. The J7 asked the J4 to provide a planner (Frank) and an engineer. The J7 provided a contractor. That became the team. The J7, a three star Army general, gathered the team together and told them their charter was to go to Hawaii and assess if the command was ready for Y2K. When they came back they were to assess whether what they saw in Hawaii could be applied to the armed forces globally. That was all the guidance they were given. Also at that time, Frank found out that he was in charge of the team. They dutifully went to Hawaii and started meeting with the planners. The only place they could find activities that had actually done some work planning for Y2K was on the installation staffs. Invariably these were civilians who had worked there for a long time and they basically said that in Hawaii and throughout PACOM they were used to operating in conditions involving typhoons, tsunamis, earthquakes and volcano eruptions. They were all very well versed in operating in conditions where electricity and water supplies were cut off and they always ensured that they had adequate back up fresh water and electricity supplied by generators. This was the case throughout the Pacific. Frank thought that was pretty good. The engineer thought that perhaps this was too simplistic and that Y2K could affect aircraft in flight or disrupt navigation equipment. Frank thought if that was the case they should shut down for the day and see what happens. There was really no way they could assess every ship and airplane with their three man team. Frank came back an filed a report that said that PACOM was prepared and that units in areas of the world not susceptible to huge natural disasters, Europe, parts of the United States, should ensure that they had generators fired up and ready to come on line at midnight to ensure continuity of operations. Much to Frank's surprise, three months later Y2K came and went without incident and Frank and his two teammates received an award from the Joint Staff J7 (a joint staff achievement medal) saying that the team was singularly responsible for fixing the Y2K crisis. Not bad for a 4 day trip with one day spent snorkeling at Hanauma Bay.

Frank also was sent with another team that was put together by the J3. The Chairman of the Joint Chiefs was asked by the United Nations to send a planning team to the United Nations to assist in planning an operation in the Congo. A team was quickly put together consisting of a lead colonel from J3 (operations), a major from J2 who incredibly had been stationed in Rwanda and had traveled extensively in the Congo and had actually travelled along the Congo River and spent time with the warlords in that vicinity, a signal Major from J6 and two J4 officers, Frank and a female colonel. The team assembled and flew up to New York that day. The chairman gave them strict orders not to cross the street. There was a US Mission to the United Nations in a building across the street from the actual UN. The mission was almost clandestine. Everyone wore civilian clothes. The mission was fairly straight forward. Frank brought his trusty G4 battle book and did all the logistical calculations for food, water, transportation, ammunitions, terrain, living areas, latrines, tents, kitchens. It was fairly routine. The other officers also provided their annexes to the plan. The team was finished within twenty four hours and the team was told that they were to brief the U.S Ambassador to the United Nations, Richard Holbrooke. There was a little dust up prior to the briefing. The team leader wanted to give the entire brief. The J4 Colonel was adamant that she would brief her portion. The team leader relented and when it came time for her to brief the Ambassador, she really put on a show. The ambassador was really impressed with the brief and he said that he wanted the team to cross the street and brief Kofi Anan.

The team leader told the Ambassador that they were not permitted to do anything but hand over the plan to the US mission and that we were to return to DC that evening. The ambassador made a few phone calls but as they were heading to the airport on a ferry from Manhattan, they were turned around. The team returned to the hotel and prepared to brief Kofi Anan the next day. While the team was in New York, an NCO stationed there got the team tickets to two Broadway plays. The team saw Les Miserable and Ms. Saigon. When Frank returned once again he received a Joint Staff award. This time it was Joint Staff Commendation medal. The citation quoted Ambassador Holbrooke saying it was the best short term contingency plan he had ever seen and that included his time spent serving in Vietnam. Frank would say he received an award for watching two Broadway plays. If this kept up, Frank would have so many medals he would look like a Dictator by the time he left the Joint Staff.

Frank's last mission on active duty was a trip with the J4 that went from the Pentagon, to PACOM in Hawaii, then Australia and finally to Korea. Frank's mission on this trip was to provide a brief on the logistical planning that was conducted during and after Operation Iraqi Freedom. Frank had been to PACOM several times and he had a few friends on the staff. Frank gave the brief and they spent one night on the town but no beach time. After one day the team boarded a commercial flight to Australia. There were two things about that flight. No one had enough miles so that all had to sit in coach due to the archaic rules in the Defense Transportation

Regulations, even though the team flew at night and were expected to work when they landed. Frank looked over at the J4 who had a laptop on the food tray and worked all night. Hard to believe executives were treated like that. The trip to Australia started in Sydney and Frank gave his brief on the first day. They day was spent in a conference room and would have lasted late into the night but there was an evening reception and dinner that the team attended. During that dinner, the Australian hosts said that would be the last day spent in a conference room. They made arrangements to have the next day's activities take place on a yacht in Sydney Harbor. The team spent the day doing some work while looking the over Sydney Harbor Bridge and the famous opera House. The next day the Australian Military flew the team to Canberra. The Joint Staff J4 had an office call with high ranking military officers and did not need the rest of the team until the afternoon. Frank had the morning off and was determined to see some wild kangaroos. He asked the workers at the hotel if there was a close place where he might get a glance of a kangaroo. They gave him directions to a local park. The park was at the base of a heavily wooded hillside. Frank figured the kangaroos would be in the woods so he walked all the way to the top of the hill without seeing anything. He started down disappointed and was standing in the park trying to figure out where he could look next. He wasn't really paying attention to his surroundings and when he tuned to leave there was a kangaroo less that two feet from him. Frank thought that kangaroos would be more like trying to see a deer in the wild, but it was more like seeing a squirrel. They were everywhere in the park. His trek up the hill was a total waste of time. In the afternoon the team laid a wreath at a monument to the Australian soldiers who lost their lives fighting in Viet Nam, a part of the war that is often overlooked in America. All Americans should watch the music video by Redgum titled "I Was Only Nineteen" that really gives a good sense of the pride and dedication of the Australian troops that fought in Vietnam.

The team then went to Korea. Fortunately, this time the team flew Qantas. The Australians hooked them up with passes to the VIP lounge and bumped them up to Business class. At least one country knew how to treat Flag officers. Upon arrival in Korea, Frank gave his brief. The J4 in Korea had served with the team when he was stationed in the Pentagon and Frank had known him for several years. The next day the J4 again had high level office call so the team had a day off. There was some unrest in Korea so the team was advised not to stray from the Dragon Hill Hotel in Yongson (Seoul, Korea). This was disappointing for Frank, who was one of the few soldiers who spent a career in the Army and did not go to Korea for a tour or an exercise. Frank's friend said it was too bad that he didn't have his class A uniform or he could go to the DMZ for a ceremony. Frank said he had his dress greens as they were worn for the ceremony in Australia. He told Frank to get on a bus that would leave at 0700 and he would spend the day at the border. Frank put on his uniform and boarded the bus with other soldiers and even some wives who were all dressed up. Frank was surprised how close the border was to Seoul. He expected to see both the South Korean and US Army on the border armed to the teeth, but he really didn't get the concept of a demilitarized zone. There was a Swedish Army unit patrolling the border with the mission to keep both sides apart as designated by the Neutral Nations Supervisory Commission. The ceremony was a Swedish Holiday and Service members and guests from all the embassies in Seoul were invited. Frank found himself on the DMZ drinking Heinekens and mingling with women in ball gowns. Not what he envisioned. He even started a conversation with a Russian Officer who had been stationed at the Russian Embassy in North Korean and now was in the South. It was a great and unexpected way to end his career.

Chapter 5
Retirement

Frank was being treated for kidney failure symptoms at Walter Reed while he was still in the military. This allowed him to continue to be treated at Walter Reed after he retired. Had he been living in virtually any location other than D.C he would have been forced to rely on the Veteran's Administration. He was in denial that there was anything wrong with his kidneys. He did have headaches caused by high blood pressure but so did everyone working in the Pentagon. In fact, Frank had a prescription for blood pressure medicine and when he asked the pharmacist if he could get if filled at the Pentagon clinic instead of going to the military hospital, the pharmacist laughed and said they bring blood pressure medicine into the Pentagon by the truckload. Whenever the doctors at Walter Reed would tell him his kidneys were failing, he would reply that he could run two miles in 14 minutes, do 70 pushups and 70 sit-ups meaning that he was in peak fitness by Army standards. For the one year prior to Frank's retirement, his nephrologist was a Navy officer, a tough guy from Philly. He told Frank that running and pushups had nothing to do with his kidneys and if he didn't change his diet and take the prescribed medicine, his kidneys would fail. He scared Frank and for as long as the doctor was treating him he made all hospital appointments and his kidney function was stable.

That doctor left and was replaced with a series of doctors. They included Frank in the decision making process and that was a mistake. Frank would not do anything unless forced to do it or scared with empirical data. One of the bad things about kidney failure is that there is not pain or outward symptoms associated with the disease. When he began the process of retiring, he took a retirement physical from the Pentagon clinic with several referrals. It was touch and go as to whether the Army would let him retire given that he had the kidney problem. To Frank, this did not make a lot of sense. He was told his kidneys were failing due to high blood pressure brought on by stress, but if he had to stay in the military the stress would only get worse. He would continue to work on the Joint Staff which was pressure filled in peace and war and by 2003 the Joint Staff and the rest of the Defense Department was functioning in a murky world between peace and war, making staff work the worst of both worlds. Also, Frank had been on the joint staff for several years and was due to rotate. He had never been in a non-deployable status and did not want to end his career that way. Fortunately, the Army medical system never quite made the connection between the physical given at the Pentagon Clinic and the kidney treatment at Walter Reed. He had to make 5 copies of his medical records during his out processing who would then forward the records to the VA. That was the first on many incomprehensible things that the VA required. Making copies of 5 things what were written by hand in 1975 and were illegible made no sense. He did not have a whole lot in his medical records and he thought about the female NCO that he had seen at Fort Belvoir who was pushing her medical records in a shopping cart because there was so much paper. He could only imagine what it was like to make 5 copies of those records. What happened to those copies is a mystery. He was told he had to make a separate appointment with the VA to take another physical with them. Since he just wanted to get out and was actually in denial that he had any long term health issues, he complied with what he was told. He scheduled an appointment with the VA and was given an appointment at a local clinic. The VA did not tell him to make an appointment. They it gave him a letter stating when his appointment was with a check for $2.40 included to cover public transportation. Frank was a retired Colonel but was treated like he could not think for himself. All of the clinical personnel treated him well. When it was time to see the doctor, the doctor treated him like he was an interruption to his day. He did not talk with him, and in fact treated him with distain. When he received the rating back from the VA signed by the VA doctor, the rating was 5 percent with no mention of a kidney issue. Having full access to faxes, emails, phones and the ability to navigate through a bureaucracy, he took the VA on. He successfully got his disability rating raised, although that process took several years. He also realized that had he had mental, financial or health problems, the system would undoubtedly have overwhelmed him. He did see the entire system improve greatly under General Shinseki.

It is still hard for Frank to believe he had kidney failure. There is a line from a Clint Eastwood movie when he is talking to a bad guy and Clint says "You won't believe what is happening to you even while it is happening." Frank had always been healthy. He worked out religiously. Being in the Army, he had to watch his weight whether he wanted to or not. The two easiest ways to fail in the Army were to fail a PT test or to be overweight. Frank would take high stress jobs and due to his personality, would make them even more stressful. There was no reason for this. Frank almost always had good bosses. They were always appreciative of what he was doing for the organization. While Frank took care of himself physically, he always had a hard time relaxing. When his son was in middle school and high school, Frank coached basketball in a recreation league and that helped him relax. High schools in Northern Virginia were large and competitive and that carried over into recreation league basketball. Many of the players were good basketball players who had staked their entire athletic hopes on making the high school basketball team. They were great players but the numbers in basketball worked against them. Usually there were only 15 kids on a team. A few slots would be taken by kids based on size alone. That left about 10 slots for schools that had over 800 kids in each grade. Another set of kids played other sports that were very demanding. The days of a kid being able to play football, basketball and baseball were basically over. It was hard to become proficient enough to be a varsity athlete in one sport and even if kids were good enough to play another sport, there just wasn't time. Regardless of the reasons, the recreation basketball program was very competitive, filled with athletes from other sports that wanted to play. Frank loved coaching. He started out as an assistant coach then got his own team for the 4 years his son was in high school. He learned the system of drafting and built a power house team. In his son's senior year his team was undefeated but did not do well in the playoffs. Frank had to go to Afghanistan but that was not the issue. One of the moms who had been to every game her son played took over and did a great job. It was just that the team started to lose players to spring sports. Other teams also began to lose players. One team lost 6 of 11 players because they were all on the varsity baseball team. Coaching was relaxing for Frank and did give him a way to get away from the pressures of work. The league required that every player play at least half the game, so it took a lot of planning to ensure that the players on the floor had a dribbler, a shooter and a rebounder at all times. After his son left high school, Frank stopped coaching and found himself with no outlet to relieve stress.

One of his coworkers asked him if he would help out during bingo night at the Springfield American Legion. He was so desperate for something to do that he agreed. Bingo was actually quite enjoyable. It was Frank's job to give money to the winners. The money was substantial. One game was for $500.00. Most games paid $50 or $100. This was a nice, relaxing outlet for Frank but it also did not last. The issue was smoking. The games were played at a rapid pace and the games needed 60 people to make a profit. The problem was that they had about 50 smokers and 50 nonsmokers who were dedicated players. Most were elderly women. Having smoke breaks was not feasible. The games were played at a rapid pace and the people who smoked basically lit one cigarette as soon as the other one was out. The bingo games eventually had to be cancelled because they could not mix the smokers with the nonsmokers. The American Legion did have a banquet for the volunteers and Frank was sitting with his wife at a large table with about 20 people. The conversation turned to hobbies. Everyone started to go around the table saying what their hobby was. Some had very exotic hobbies like working with stained glass or restoring a 1967 Mustang. All had something. As the conversation moved closer to Frank, he was wracking his brain. The only thing he did was work, go to the gym and go home. He liked to watch the Pittsburgh Steelers and he liked to walk the dog, but those hardly seemed like hobbies. He realized that he had nothing and when it came his turn that is what he said: "I've got nothing". He realized that was not a healthy way to go through life. That weekend he went to the local Harley Dealer and bought a Harley Sportster. He never again wanted to be in a position where he could not point to at least one thing he did that was not related to work.

Chapter 6
Iraq

Frank was able to get a contractor position and continue to do the planning work that he was doing on active duty. He worked on site on the Joint Staff. In the short time between when he retired (essentially a few months after the fall of Baghdad in 2003) and he began working as a contractor, the war in Iraq was turning from an occupation into a counter insurgency with potential to escalate into a civil war. Frank became involved in identifying units that would rotate into both Iraq and Afghanistan as it became clear that forces would be required for an extended period of time. Frank was already well versed in the Request for Forces Process and he had written a paper on mobilization while he was in the Industrial College of the Armed Forces so he began attending sourcing conferences that ensured that units were manned, trained and equipped in time to rotate into the theater in order to replace similar units that were coming up on a 12 month rotation. This was exacting work but Frank enjoyed it. There were challenges everywhere but sourcing logistical units was challenging because most of the force structure was in the Reserves. Fortunately these units were well trained and ready. Equipping was not a real problem as most units could fall in on equipment already in theater.

Frank was asked to be part of a team that was led by the Joint

Staff J4 to go to the theater and assess the adequacy of the up armored program that had been established to mitigate the effects of improvised explosive devices and to determine what if any functions could be contracted out. Incredibly for Frank it was the first time he had gone to Iraq. He did not go there while on active duty although he had been close (Kuwait and Turkey several times). The trip was a whirlwind moving quickly throughout the theater on a dedicated C130. They visited Balad, where Frank linked up with his Fort Bragg comrades who were providing logistical support to the entire Iraqi theater. They also visited the Marines it Al Assad. The Marines really took security seriously. Frank had been offered a weapon while in Kuwait but did not take one. He figured that if something happened there would be plenty of weapons around. In fact, since he was on a team from the Joint Staff, team members from the other services were given weapons but it had been years, and in one case, the team member had never fired the weapon. Everywhere the team went they were escorted by a ring of Marines. Since they were a logistical team, the Marines were adamant that we see the Marine Logisticians in action at Al Taquaddam. The team was scheduled to travel by ground but that would have meant getting close to Fallujah where a full scale battle was being waged. The decision was made to fly and land on the airstrip at Al Taqquadam. The plane probably taxied longer than it flew but it was well worth the trip to see what the Marines were doing to support forces fully committed in combat. They had established connectivity that allowed them to monitor stock statuses in real time. It was very impressive and well worth the trip. The team left Iraq and went to Qatar then Afghanistan and returned to write up a report. The team wasn't back in the Pentagon for a week when the OEF Commander said they wanted to do a slightly different study and wanted someone from the J4 team to be part of a theater team that would also be headed up by a three star general only in this case an Army General. A Marine Colonel on the Joint Staff who was on the team volunteered to go but since he did not work full time in sourcing, Frank requested to attend also. Frank and the Colonel linked up at Dulles and got ready for the thirteen hour flight that they would be spending in coach. Frank was 6 foot four, so sleep or relaxation was out of the question. Upon arrival in Kuwait, they were met by a driver who took them to the massive base in the Kuwaiti desert known as Camp Arifjan. Frank expected to get a room in the barracks complex known as Building I. He might even swing a VIP room like the last trip. He was surprised when they drove past the barracks and headed for the tent city in zone 6. The driver told Frank to pay attention as they passed a shower trailer. Even though it was still about a mile till they would get to the tents where they would be staying, the male shower trailer in that area was broken. Not only were they staying in tents, they were staying in a rundown area of the tent city reserved for soldiers and civilians who were only staying for short while before heading to Iraq. It was almost midnight when the driver dropped them off. The tent Frank was staying in was flapping in the wind. Frank and the Colonel however, were the only occupants. The driver said he would be back at 0400 with weapons and body armor and would take them to the airfield.

There were some females in an adjacent tent who were standing in the stone pathway outside the tent in their pajamas. Frank walked down and struck up a conversation with the women. One of the ladies seemed to be about 70 years old. The reason she looked like a grandmother was because she was a grandmother. She was an employee of the Army Air Force Exchange System and she volunteered to work in the PX that was being established in Balad. It was hard to believe the US was sending grandmothers to a combat zone, but she was ready for whatever may happen. She said she loved the soldiers and wanted to make the deployment a little better and she was willing to go to Iraq to do this.

The Marine and Frank got about two hours of sleep and were standing outside their tents ready to go when the driver showed up, Frank was not offered a weapon this time They showed up at the airfield and the specialist who was building the manifests stated that they were in for a treat. They were going to fly to Baghdad in a Sherpa. Frank was in the Army for 28 years but he had never seen or heard of a Sherpa. They walked out to the plane and were met by a sixty-five year old crew chief. Frank was starting to think that the war was manned by AARP. The crew chief started to give a safety brief; Frank and the Colonel were starting to have second thoughts about this mode of transportation. The plane was a twenty foot shipping container with wings on the side and a bullet shaped cockpit in front. It certainly did not look air worthy, and the briefing by the sergeant crew chief did little to inspire confidence. The mission for the plane was to transport a helicopter engine to Baghdad to fix a helicopter that was AOG (aircraft on ground). The passengers were going as opportune cargo. The crew chief started by showing the passengers the unit patch that he and the pilots had sewn on their uniforms. The unit motto was " Unarmored, Unarmed and Unafraid". He stated that there were no offensive weapons on the aircraft, no rockets, no machine gun, nothing. There were also no defensive countermeasures. No flares, no chafe, no obscurants. He said that the plane was hard to maneuver, but not to worry because the unit was from the Alaska National Guard and all members of the unit were bush pilots and they were unrivalled in the abilities as pilots and crew. He told the passengers that they would go to a cruising altitude of 10,000 ft. Unfortunately the plane was not pressurized. The pilots and the crew would have oxygen bottles, but since this plane was designed for cargo there were no amenities like oxygen for the passengers. He also said it would be cold, so we should put on our snivel gear. Essentially we would be experiencing the same weather and oxygen level if were climbing to the top of a mountain in Colorado. Then he said when we get about 30 minutes outside of Baghdad, the plane will drop down to nap of the earth for the approach in. He said we would drop so quickly that the goal was to rupture at least one passenger's eardrums. He also said we would be so low that the kids would throw rocks at the plane and hit us. They boarded the plane. On board was a young guy who was an Army Air Force Exchange System employee and an older guy who worked for KBR. Frank and the Colonel rounded out the manifest. The two civilians were wearing jeans, T shirts, body armor and a helmet. Frank assumed that all Americans in a war zone would be in a uniform like he was that clearly identified them as noncombatants in accordance with the Geneva Convention. Evidently that did not apply here. The most important passenger on the flight was an engine that was strapped into the middle of the plane. They took off and quickly went to 10000 ft. The crew chief was hitting on the oxygen, but lack of oxygen was hardly a bother for the passengers. The flight was only about ninety minutes and, as promised, at the one hour mark the plane dropped like it was shot out of the sky. The passengers were furiously chewing gum to keep their eardrums intact. It was hard to tell how low the plane was, but it appeared to be about 50 feet. This tactic prevented engagement by missiles but did leave the plane vulnerable to small arms fire. To combat this the pilot took evasive action which was quite impressive considering he was flying a plane whose fuselage was as high as it was wide and essentially created the least aerodynamic shape that could be designed. They landed without incident at what was Baghdad international airport. They climbed off the ramp and saw an eclectic mix of helicopters, fighter jets and cargo planes one of which had the rising sun of Japan. Incredibly there was also a cargo jet that was missing its back door. Well welcome to Iraq.

Frank and the Marine Colonel linked up with the Army guys. It was a good team that worked well together. The General was little concerned that the Joint Staff prima donnas would leak findings back to the Pentagon. He made it quite clear that that better not occur and they assured him they had no intention of reporting anything back to the Pentagon. Frank had served with most of the team members and they assured the General there would not be an issue. This trip was not C130 flights to large bases. The team loaded up on helicopters and flew to every brigade sized base in Iraq. Frank had not spent a lot of time in helicopters. He spent 11 years in Germany and three years in the Airborne but was not air assault qualified. Even as a civilian he was decked out in body armor, a helmet and web gear. As the team loaded onto two helicopters, Frank was the last to get in. He was trying to get settled when the helicopter took off and banked sharply. Frank was looking for a waist safety belt not realizing the helicopter had a shoulder harness. Fortunately the female Lieutenant Colonel grabbed him and helped him with the seat belt. The only casualty was his sun glasses, a nice pair of Oakley's that fell to the tarmac. Frank vowed never be to be last on the helicopter again so on the way back he changed places with the female Lieutenant Colonel. This put him in an even worse situation. The helicopter flew with the doors open and sitting in the back row facing the pilot on the second seat from the door meant that a 130 MPH prop blast was hitting the passenger in the face for the entire trip. No matter how he tried to time his entrance into the helicopters, he always seemed to get this seat. The trips were miserable but the experience of flying to every base in the country and hearing the challenges was a great learning experience. They wrote a very detailed concept of support that in Franks opinion reduced the logistics footprint, while enhancing security. The results were presented to the theater commander while the team was in country and were immediately implemented.

Chapter 7

The Airborne

Up until that point, the highlight of Frank's career had been an assignment as a commander in the XVIII Airborne Corps. Frank was part of an experiment that the Army was running to mix up the experiences of the officers they were putting in command. Frank attended jump school immediately after graduating from Officer Candidate School which was essentially just across the street. Frank was a stick leader and the stick he was in charge of happened to be the other service members who were attending jump school. He had Navy SEALs, Marine Force Recon and Air Force Para Rescue. Unlike the Army soldiers, who were fresh out of basic training, these service members had all went through a rigorous in service program. That still did not prevent Frank from having to do 10 pushups for each soldier during the pre-dawn first inspection. That was thirty times ten pushups in the first ten minutes of every day. To say it was pre-dawn was a misnomer. Frank attended jump school in August and the day started at 3:00 am and ended at 1100 in the morning in an attempt to beat the heat and humidity. Frank's stick (the term given to a group of jumpers that would line up on one side of an aircraft and exit together) had two female black hat instructors. They did not feel the need to prove they were tougher than the male black hats. They both exuded confidence and were incredibly physically fit. They were quite a sight with their black hats, white T shirts and blue shorts way above their combat boots. Of course their legs were tanned and muscular and during breaks Frank would be daydreaming while looking at the smooth white hair barely visible on their thighs. It made jump school almost bearable. When it got real hot, the guys would take their shirts off. This turned out to be more of a hassle than a relief. The airborne trainees would do pushups, sit ups and leg lifts in a wood chip filled exercise area. After an unbearable length of time, all students would go thru the showers that were set up outside. After getting soaked, they would hustle back to the exercise pit where the wood chips would stick to everything especially any gaps between the torso and the fatigue pants. It made everyone completely miserable. This would go on all morning, culminating four mile run. Frank graduated from jump school and while he enjoyed the exercises and the sense of being elite, he realized he really wasn't good at it. By the time he figured out which way the wind was blowing and pulled his risers to create a windbreak to slow down, the wind would change and Frank, already screaming to the ground and because of his height and weight, would hit even harder because he pulled the wrong slip. After graduation, he had no interest in serving in an airborne unit. Eighteen years later, he was selected to command an airborne logistical battalion at Fort Bragg as part of the XVIII Airborne Corps. He was fortunate to be prepositioned at Fort Bragg for a year allowing him to get used to the jumping. He was also fortunate he stayed in shape so the extra running that came with an assignment to Fort Bragg assignment did not bother him. He attended the basic airborne refresher course on the 82d Airborne side of the post. The day of his refresher class happened to be the same day that a sniper opened fire on a formation of soldiers in a stadium across the street from the refresher training. The soldiers in the refresher training could hear the yelling but did not think too much about it.

Approximately twenty minutes after the sniper had fired, the black hat instructor told the class that there was a sniper shooting people across the road. Twenty minutes later he said the sniper was caught. They did not miss a minute of training.

Frank's first jump was uneventful other than it was a Hollywood jump (no pack or weapon) and as he exited the aircraft his legs went way up above his head and for a second, Frank thought he was going to do a backwards somersault, but gravity eventually brought his legs down and his chute opened. He actually had a good landing and, like all paratroopers, was so high on adrenaline that all he wanted to do that night was get drunk and get a tattoo. His second jump was not as smooth. Since he was on the staff as opposed to command, he was way back in the plane and would jump on the third pass. As he exited the aircraft, he did not tuck his chin into his chest and the risers ripped across his neck and ears then wrenched his helmet right off his head. As he looked straight ahead he could see the helmet spinning in front of him. It had hurt so bad that at first he thought he might have been decapitated. But then he looked up and saw the canopy was open, so he started to look for a soft place to land. That was a problem. This jump was part of a heavy drop with the Corps Artillery and they had dropped their M198 howitzers ahead of the jump and now they were scattered all over the drop zone. Since it was the third and last pass, trucks on the chute detail were driving across the drop zone picking up chutes. The medics were also driving in their ambulance looking for injured jumpers. From 500 feet Above Ground Level (AGL), the drop zone looked like Times Square. There did not appear to be a safe place to land. Additionally two jumpers next to him had become entangled. That happens when one jumper moves directly under another jumper stealing his air and causing the chute of the jumper above him to collapse. That is what happened and the top jumper fell though the lower jumper's chute and now was hanging on to the other jumpers risers with both dropping very quickly. Frank ended up landing close to a howitzer, but did not hit it. He also did a fairly good parachute landing fall and did not hit his head. As soon as he got out of his chute, the COSCOM Commander, a Brigadier General, drove up in his HMMWV and started chewing him out. Frank explained that his helmet fell off during the exit. The COSCOM Commander was later assigned with Frank on the Joint Staff at the Pentagon and he loved to tell the story of the helmetless Lieutenant Colonel wandering around Sicily Drop Zone. His next jump was not much better. It was an afternoon jump and Frank was the second jumper out of the left door. He could have been first but Frank did not like being the first jumper. Most soldiers considered it an honor so Frank would usually get soldier who had just reenlisted or gotten promoted to jump first as a reward. In any event Frank went out the door and started heading for the edge of the drop zone. The only thing in site was one HMMWV that was being used by the safeties. Frank was heading right for it. He tried his best to maneuver away from the HMMWV but the chute kept him on a collision course. Frank was sure he was going to hit it and accepted that maybe the canvas of the roof would break his fall. Then he noticed that a ladder was stretched across the top. The ladder was required in case a soldier got stuck in a tree and could not get down. Frank realized that the ladder could, in fact, be what breaks his fall and the envisioned on of the rungs stopping his momentum with his crotch as both legs went through either side. Frank closed his eyes and prepared for impact. To his surprise, he landed on the sand next to the HMMMWV and his chute collapsed over the open passenger side door. Frank questioned the safeties why didn't they move the vehicle as he was the only one in the area and surely they saw him. They replied in unison that they saw him but if they moved the vehicle and a jumper hit it, it was their fault. If the jumper hit a stationary vehicle, it was the jumpers fault. One of the Safeties asked Frank if he was the number one jumper. Frank said he was the number 2. The safety said he would put that in his report and that Frank would probably help the pilot get promoted as the HMMWV was the personnel point of impact and Frank had landed as close as humanely possible. Once more the paratroopers did not use any flexibility when implementing the rules and that was a good thing.

The COSCOM commander had met Frank on his first day at the COSCOM and invited Frank to a softball practice in preparation for a game against the NCOs. Frank was certainly a good enough athlete to excel in a softball game with a bunch of officers. At that practice, Frank was playing second base and the general was playing shortstop. The general asked if Frank had played basketball in college. Frank said he played football at a small college. In the General's mind that meant he was an all American from Penn State. Frank did not say anything to dispute or support this. He didn't say he played club football and that no scholarships were offered and the team was barely able to garner 22 people together for a practice.

At one point in Frank's command tour, the COSCOM was offered the opportunity to get British jump wings. That involved one day of training with British jumpmasters and one jump using a British chute. The COSCOM was given an entire Saturday which meant several flights. They would be Hollywood jumps with no weapon or rucksack and no 55 minute flight prior to the drop. The Friday training was uneventful. It seemed they used the same procedures and almost spoke the same language (although the paras were mostly tough little guys with severe cockney accents). The Brits did say their chute opened quickly and could actually be dropped from 250 feet Above the Ground Level (AGL). The chutes also used what the U.S paratroopers called the dial of death release mechanism. U.S. paratroopers had used this in the past, but now had a ring release mechanism that allowed one set of risers to be released by pulling down hard on the ring. It worked fairly well. Again, no one thought the release would be a big deal. They wanted to get the British Jump wings so they could wear them on their dress uniforms. As the jumpers assembled on Green Ramp on Saturday morning it was brutally hot. Everyone was praying for a breeze. The jumpers donned the chutes and were inspected by the British jumpmasters. The group that Frank was in sat on green ramp for about an hour until it was their turn to load. Even though Frank was a battalion commander, there was essentially no rank on this jump. The British were in charge and everyone was just a jumper. Frank was the number 18 of 32 jumpers on the left side. They got up in the plane and fastened themselves into their seats (cargo nets actually). As soon as they got airborne, the British jumper had the outboard personnel stand up. There was not enough room for both the jumpers on both sides of the plane to stand up at once. What had to happen was that one side stood up on their seats. Then the other side stood up placed their seats in the stowed position. Then the other side got down and placed their seats in the stowed position. As soon as this happened the jumpmaster said 10 minutes till drop. It was incredibly hot in the plane and there was a commotion in the back. One of the female lieutenants had passed out from the heat. This information was passed to the British jumpmaster and he directed that the lieutenant who had passed out be moved to the front. She was. He directed that all personnel hook up their static lines and check equipment. When that was done he opened the door. He then, grabbed her by the collar and held her head out the door for a few seconds. The plane had slowed down but was still going 130 miles per hour. After a few gulps of fresh air at 130 miles per hour, she was wide awake. The jumpmaster called one minute, and then thirty seconds then the green light came on. The jumpmaster threw her out the door then everyone else followed. Frank had no problem exiting the aircraft, but noticed that the female major on the other side of the plane came underneath the plane an in front of Frank moving like she was shot out of a cannon. Frank's chute opened and he looked up and couldn't believe what he saw. Instead of a canopy, the chute looked like a Frisbee. It was almost flat. No wonder it could be used from 250 feet. It opened quickly but it hardly gathered any air. It was also clear now why all the British Paratroopers were little guys (to include a few Ghurkas). Frank knew that this chute would not be enough for his 220 lbs. He also noticed that while there was no breeze at green ramp, the winds had really picked up over the drop zone. The safeties on the ground were very liberal with the wind readings because everyone wanted the British jump wings. No one was supposed to jump if the winds were more than 13 miles per hour, but that did not really consider gusts or winds at altitude. In any event, everyone was out of the aircraft and heading for the ground. At least Frank was dropping straight down. Some of the lighter jumpers were being carried off into the trees. When Frank finally realized the wind was really blowing hard, he tried to determine the direction and pull the risers in the direction of the wind. It didn't do much, but at least in theory slowed you down. Frank didn't get the direction correct or perhaps the wind changed but he pulled the wrong slip and instead of bracing against the wind, the chute now acted as a sail and gathered wind increasing speed as he hit the ground. Frank slammed into the ground hip first. A parachute landing fall is supposed to follow a prescribed order beginning with the balls of the feet first, then calf, then twisting to the thigh, then the backside (infamous fourth point of contact), then flip the legs over and roll on the upper shoulder. That was the theory. A lot of people would hit feet, knees, face or feet, backside head. As long as your feet hit first, however, you would likely walk away, the standard for a jump (any one you can walk away from is a success). On this jump, Frank hit his left hip first and he knew he would be hurting for a long time. When he landed, he tried to get out of the harness using the dial of death. Incredibly, Frank was being dragged. He had never experienced this because he weighed over 200 pounds. Eventually, he was able to turn the dial and release the harness. When he stood up he could not believe what he was seeing. Virtually every chute on the ground was open and dragging a jumper along the ground. It looked like the Oklahoma land rush with prairie schooners going across the drop zone. Frank and a few others started to grab and step on chutes and help jumpers get out of the chutes. While he was doing that, he watched one jumper oscillating severely in the way down. The jumper hit on his tailbone on the field landing strip. The field landing strip was a runway embedded into the drop zone that allowed the Air Force to practice landing on unimproved runways. The field landing strip was soaked with creosote and it could be argued that it was harder than cement. Jumpers tried to avoid it at all costs, but given winds and the canopy type chutes, often the landing strip could not be avoided. The jumper broke his tailbone upon landing. He was unable to get out of his chute and was being dragged along the landing strip. He had flipped over and now his face was smashed along the landing strip, practically separating his nose from his face. Frank helped him get out of his chute. It was the worst thing Frank had ever seen on the drop zone. Blood was everywhere, and Frank didn't even realize that his tailbone was broken. The medics were busy that day. Everyone truly earned their British jump wings. Frank felt so bad about the injured jumper that he went to visit him at Womack hospital at Fort Bragg.

That was not Frank's worst experience on an airborne operation. That came on an operation where he didn't even get a chance to jump. Jumps can be called off in mid-flight for a number of reasons, but typically involve weather i.e. lighting or high winds. Rain could be a factor. Paratroopers could jump in the rain but there were only so many drying towers on Fort Bragg so often jumpers were told that they could not jump in the rain because there was no capability to dry out the chutes. Jumps were called off in flight fairly often, but had never happened to Frank. He was on one jump where everyone had loaded on to the aircraft and were seated ready to go. When the pilot cranked up the four engines on the C130, one of the engines made a popping sound that sounded like a small explosion. The plane quickly filled with smoke. The paratroopers just sat there waiting for someone in the Air Force to tell them what to do. There were strange rules that allowed the Army to fly on these missions for free but they had to do everything the Air Force said and meet all Air Force requirements or the Army would be charged for the flight and that was a sin that would not be tolerated at Fort Bragg. Finally an Air Force loadmaster shouted into a bullhorn that one of the engines was smoking "More than usual". Certainly it was not uncommon for a C130 to be leaking fluid and smoking out of one or more of the four engines, but this was beyond a routine deficiency. The paratroopers exited the aircraft and had to stay fully outfitted on green ramp while one airman with a small ladder and a flashlight peered into the engine for twenty minutes before announcing that the mission was scrubbed.

On the mission that was called off in flight, it was apparent the winds were way beyond the acceptable range. Frank was the Airborne Commander. He went to the weather decision brief. For the Army, there was no decision. If the plane was flying, the paratroopers would be along for the ride. The plane took off and flew the requisite fifty-five minutes. It was really windy and the pilot was making incredibly sharp turns. Again this was also training for the pilot and some took this training more serious than others. This pilot was really into the evasive maneuvers and that, coupled with the high winds, made for a miserable 55 minutes for all in the back. When jumpmaster gave the troopers the ten minute warning, the first stick stood up and got ready to jump. There would be three passes if all went well, so on each pass about 12 jumpers would exit from each side of the aircraft. The jumpers stood for ten minutes but as they passed the drop zone the light stayed red and no one was able to jump. The plane did a ten minute racetrack maneuver and the second set of jumpers stood up, hooked up and got ready to jump. Once again, the light stayed red and no one jumped. The third pass became very chaotic. All jumpers were now up and hooked up, but were not passing the all okay up to the jumpmaster. The jumpers are all required to perform checks on their equipment and on the equipment on the jumper in from of them. The jumpmaster then says sound off for equipment check and the last jumper is taps the jumper in front of him on the thigh and say "Okay", until this is passed to the number one jumper who says "All Okay Jumpmaster". For some reason, this was not happening. Now it would have been easy to assume that all was okay, and it would have been even easier to assume that there would be no jump on the third pass, but paratroopers never take shortcuts. The safety officer on this mission was a lieutenant from the brigade staff. He took it upon himself to literally fight his way from the front of the plane to the back and he personally checked every jumper's equipment and static line. By the time he got back to the front the jumpmaster was already giving the one minute warning. It was a fine example of leadership. By this time, the jumpers on the first pass has been standing for thirty minutes, being buffeted by the winds in the aircraft and most were feeling very woozy. Only going out the door frees the paratroopers from all the weight he or she is carrying. In this case, it could be well over 100 lbs. Frank had a six foot four frame to distribute the weight and he was hurting and he could only imagine what some of the smaller jumpers were feeling, especially those carrying the M60 Machine Gun or other extra weight. The plane made the final pass and the light stayed red. Frank has no idea what would happen next. The loadmaster closed the door and told everyone to unhook their static lines and sit down on the floor. The seats were already stowed and there was not time to put them back into position so that the jumpers could sit down and fasten their seat belts. The jumpers tried as best as they could to sit down with their packs and weapons but clearly there was not enough room for all. The pilot, still looking for training opportunities, began a corkscrew landing. Now that the Army is in combat, everyone is aware of a corkscrew landing, but to the jumpers on that flight, it seemed like we were in a spin ala Maverick and Goose from Top Gun. Most were sure they were crashing. Of course there are no windows and only a few red dome lights were turned on giving the plane an eerie glow. The plane quickly dropped and hit the runway with a huge thud and bounced straight back up in the air. All of the paratroopers in the back went flying. Again most thought they had crashed. The plane bounced again this time not quite as high and some paratroopers' actually thought they might survive. The plane quickly screeched to a halt and the loadmaster let the ramp down. There were a lot of bloody noses and bruises but not real injuries. Seeing the runway when the ramp was dropped was like participating in a miracle. Frank never wanted to experience anything like that again.

As Frank was about to leave command he had a final jump. This jump was part of an evaluation and Frank's unit was being evaluated with an MP unit and a medical unit. Frank once again was placed back in the aircraft. This was because they had dropped a few HMMWVs that belonged to the battalion. In theory, the jumpers would land near the equipment because of the way they were cross loaded on the plane. Frank was between two MP enlisted soldiers. When they were hooked up and waiting for the green light, the soldier in front of Frank turned and said have a good jump, see you on the ground. Frank did the same to the soldier behind him. The thing that made airborne troopers special was that all shared the dangers and hardships. No one could jump for you, no matter what the rank. You knew you could count on fellow jumpers no matter what happened on the ground. The jump was at dawn on Salerno drop zone. Frank once again was heading for a bad landing. In this case he hit feet, knees then face. In fact, the last thing he remembered thinking was that at least it was Salerno drop zone and that drop zone was known for the soft sand. Frank landed, got out of his chute and even took a leak. That was all automatic. Then he looked around and started to wonder why he wasn't in his bed. Also the last thing he remembered was it was dark and now it was brightly lit. He must be just waking up in the morning, but he wasn't at home in bed. He had certainly received a concussion. He wasn't totally knocked out but he had no idea where he was. His S-3, a Captain, walked by and asked him if he had a good jump. Frank had to say he was a little disoriented. He had no idea where he was. His S3 helped him with his chute and took him to see the medics. By the time he made it to the medics, he had recovered. There really wasn't much concern about concussions at that time, so Frank answered a few simple questions and was sent on this way. That would be his last jump and was clearly not the way Frank wanted to end his airborne career.

Chapter 8
JRTC and Live Fire

The major training event for the Airborne and light Brigades was a rotation to the Joint Readiness Training Center at Fort Polk Louisiana. Logistics units from the COSCOM typically deployed with the brigades to ensure that the exercise did not get bogged down with logistics. These units provided what was called echelon above brigade logistics support and it was a tactical operation that replicated the intense missions and evaluations that the brigade in the maneuver box underwent to include the Brigades internal Logistics support battalion. Typically, echelon above brigade logistics units were assigned a lead observer controller but other evaluators were drawn from like units at home station. Also the COSCOM deployed as a Task Force and normally did not include the Battalion Commander and staff. Frank had been the senior evaluator for two battalion (both off post). In fact the unit he evaluated at 101st was a superb unit and evaluating them turned out to be a great learning experience for Frank and the commanders and staff that assisted in the evaluation. When Frank's unit was tapped to go to JRTC to support one of the Brigades it was determined that the battalion would deploy with the battalion commander and a skeleton staff. He also was fully integrated into all aspects of the Airborne Brigades planning. A sister battalion commander asked

Frank if he could deploy his bulldozer from his ammunition company to JRTC. Frank balked at this. The bulldozer was a pain for light units. It had to be loaded on a low boy and dragged around the battlefield, but the battalion commander said he really wanted to have a chance to use the bulldozer as it was intended. Frank relented and took the bulldozer. It turned out to be the best decision he ever made. Frank's battalion ended up on the other side of the post near a large field hospital and was fairly far removed from the airborne brigade. The training was intense and the weather added to the challenge. It rained nonstop for three straight days and at one point, three of Frank's 5000 gallon fuel tankers slid off the dirt road and down a steep hill. Fortunately they did not roll over but they could not get out. The bulldozer operator sprang into action and immediately pulled them back to higher ground. Frank had always had healthy respect for tracked vehicles from his days in Germany as an enlisted soldier and this only reinforced it. The bulldozer also cut roads, dug in the TOC, and made an eminently defensible main gate to the area. Frank's support Operations Officer said the operator could use that blade like it was a spatula. Frank would always say without that bulldozer his equipment might still be at Fort Polk.

Near the end of the exercise, the airborne brigade was tasked to conduct an active defense against the professional opposing force that was permanently stationed at Fort Polk. They were aggressive and had an intimate knowledge of the terrain. Frank was invited to meet with the Brigade Commander and the Infantry Battalion Commanders at his TOC. The original plan was to sling class IV barrier material that was loaded on flat racks to the defensive positions using three Chinook helicopters, but after three weeks of intense training the Chinooks were down for maintenance. Frank stated that he could send a platoon of Palletized Load System trucks to pick up the flat racks and deliver them. He could see that no one was enthused with this idea. The airborne Infantry specialized in stealth and having huge trucks from the COSCOM wandering around their area would surely giveaway their positions. Frank said that all the drivers and assistant drivers were airborne qualified and that he would send a good lieutenant and platoon sergeant to ensure that the soldiers remained focused on tactics. He did not mention that about one fourth were female. The commanders were not convinced, but they did not have any other options. When the trucks arrived, the battalion commanders were absolutely amazed at what the soldiers, both male and female, could do with the trucks and flat racks. These trucks did not require forklifts and the driver could drop the flat rack without ever leaving the cab. In fact, where the helicopters could only drop the flat racks in certain drop zones or clearings, these trucks could drop the flat racks exactly where the battalion commanders wanted them. It reduced the time to emplace the barriers by hours. Additionally, the trucks had ring mounted fifty cals, Mark 19s and M60 machine guns, effectively doubling the firepower available to the infantry. While Frank did not state that the trucks could be used for defense, he assumed he would not see those trucks until the exercise was over and he was fine with that. The exercise ended on a high note and the Brigade Commander took the time to write a note to the COSCOM Commander praising the great support provided during the rotation.

It was excellent training for the units, but the COSCOM Commander did not believe it adequately prepared the entire for combat so External Evaluations were conducted at home station. This began with an alert and a parachute assault by the airborne portion of the unit, a rail move, a convoy to the Port of Morehead City where equipment was loaded onto an Army vessel, moved to an unimproved port offloaded and convoyed back to Fort Bragg. That was followed by an intense 10 day exercise that required the unit to defend against an enemy while given real and simulated support missions. The 10 day exercise was intense with AARs at the end of each day. Also beneficial was that the evaluators were drawn from within the COSCOM. Normally the evaluation took place at the beginning of the commander's second year in command.

Also the XVIIII Airborne Corps required live fires be conducted for all units not just the combat units. This differed from scripted ranges in that platoons would deploy to the live fire range with all weapons (M16s, M203s, 50 Cals, Mark 19s, Claymores) and it was the platoon leaders' job to place the weapons and then integrate supporting fire from artillery and even helicopter gunship support. This was new to most logistics units. Frank thought it was superb. Every time he went to the field he made it a point to ask the platoon leaders what was the thought process behind where they had placed their weapons. Within 10 seconds he could determine how much if any thought was put into weapons placement and security. Certainly all lieutenants had been trained in this. He emphasized that logistics units have enough fire power to defeat virtually any threat. They certainly could defend against light infantry and Special Forces; in fact anything short of armor units could be defeated with an integrated approach to defense. Frank was not looking for a text book solution, just an integration of the weapons systems and placement based on the terrain and likely avenues of approach. The live fire provided the perfect opportunity to demonstrate this. Also the live fire required that a Battalion Commander be on site for every rotation of platoons. Frank was the senior battalion Commander in the Brigade and he was appointed to be on site for the rotation of every platoon, regardless of what battalion they originated from. It was superb training for the battalion commander as well as the platoon leaders and NCOs. Many of the NCOs had served in the 82d Airborne and a lot had started their careers in the infantry. Several officers were branch detailed to combat arms and had participated in live fires. This training gave each platoon the opportunity to achieve the highest level of training. Frank also became much more tactically proficient as he watched the platoons roll through. He learned from the lieutenants and sergeants and they could learn from him. He also required the Company commander to stay with him in a make shift Tactical Operations Center he set up on the range with members of his own S-3 section. The Company Commanders were there to observe and conduct AARs, not take over. The live fire took place over 7 days rolling 22 platoons through the range. It was fantastic.

Since the live fire worked so well, the XVIII ABC also established a convoy live fire range on Fort Bragg. This was run the same way. Platoons were directed to roll through with a Battalion Commander on site to manage the training. Frank volunteered to conduct this range as well. Once again, all 22 platoons rolled through the training. One of the Commanders was so confident in his platoons that he requested they go through the range at night. Frank agreed only after observing the platoon in the daylight. Each convoy would encounter an obstacle and it was up to the platoon to have a plan to breech the obstacle. Some of the platoons really excelled at this. Like most things, it required preplanning and rehearsal. In fact, Frank observed his Laundry and Bath unit conducting try outs to be a member of the breech team. It was headed up by the motor sergeant and he would conduct tryouts weekly. It was like the try outs for the band positions in the movie Drumline. Anyone in the company could challenge for a position. Frank saw the sergeant cut a member of the breach team for lack of hustle. The troops really took to this training. It was not without danger or harrowing moments. Frank had to ride in one of the vehicles as it went through the course. These trucks would have six or eight soldiers in the back with various types of weapons to address threats that would pop up on either side of the convoy. (mostly targets that could simulate weapons firing). Also many of the trucks had ring mounted crew served weapons. The platoon could really get a good idea of how lethal they could be. They certainly were not defenseless trucks moving through combat zones. Again, given planning and training, they could be able to defeat anything short of tanks that they may encounter. Frank also could get a good feel for the maintenance of the weapons. Sometimes there were more rounds ejected in the bed of the truck due to jams than were fired down range. Frank also noted real excellence. One of the guys in the back of a truck was manning an M60 and he and his assistant gunner could really make the machine gun hum. They could lay down suppression fire that would overcome even the most determined enemy. Frank recognized the soldier as someone that was about to get discharged due to alcohol issues. Frank decided right then and there to give the soldier another chance. In Frank's estimation, this soldier had the misfortune of joining the Army during peacetime. Frank talked to him after the exercise and begged him to stay straight. He also recommended that the soldier transfer to Kuwait or another assignment where there less temptation. Frank only had a few months left in command and he was not sure what happened to the soldier but if the battalion had to deploy, this guy was going to be one of the first on the manifest list.

Chapter 9
Haiti, Bosnia and Israel

Frank's tour at Fort Bragg was essentially a peacetime tour, however he did deploy a maintenance company under his command to Bosnia and a maintenance and supply element under his command to Haiti. The unit that deployed to Haiti was sent almost as soon as Frank had assumed command. The invasion that was called off in mid-flight had happened about three months prior. The Army had provided the Haitians with tons of equipment, but did not put in place any means to manage it. It is fair to say that the United States underestimated just how poor a country that Haiti was and that any influx of material would feed directly into a black market. Frank was told to send a team down and get a handle on the CUCV situation. The CUCV was a strange case that epitomized what the Army would do during peacetime to save money. The CUCV was a Chevy Blazer. Why someone thought this would be a good for use as a combat vehicle was beyond comprehension. It had way too much glass to operate in environments that the Army operated in. It even had a rear window that could be lowered electronically. This would break instantly. The Army finally fielded the HMMWV to replace it. This vehicle was designed specifically for the military and it least it made sense in that it could operate off road. Since the Army had a glut of CUCVs, a decision was made to give them to the

Haitian national police to use. Frank was told that they had given the Haitian police 2,500 CUCVs. After two months, most could not be accounted for and of those, only a small percentage were operational. Frank was told to send an accountable officer and a team of mechanics to Haiti to set up a property book to account for the vehicles and to establish a motor pool to dispatch and maintain the vehicles. Frank immediately sent a team under the direction of a strong, jumpmaster qualified lieutenant and a great NCO to Haiti to get the situation under control. It was hard work to turn this mind set around and required cooperation from the highest levels of the Haitian police force, but the lieutenant was able to get a handle on the accountability of the vehicles and even managed to get a few back that had been sold on the black market. The maintenance of the vehicles was not a problem. Frank had sent expert mechanics to Haiti, but they had to admit they had never met better mechanics that those in Haiti. There is no such thing as a junk yard in Haiti. Anything of value that can be repaired is repaired. The mechanics were hard working and industrious. When the Haitian mechanics were supplied with repair parts and tools, it was like they were in a dream world. The readiness rates of the CUCVs never dipped below ninety percent. There was some danger in the assignment, but that was mostly due to the poverty. There was not a real threat from any organized insurrection.

Frank kept in close touch with his lieutenant and planned to visit his troops on Thanksgiving. At Fort Bragg, he was told he had to go to the Military Intelligence unit and get a counter terrorism briefing, which he did. The briefer told him not to do anything that would make him recognizable as an American. Frank said he would try his best and promised not to wear his Pittsburgh Steeler windbreaker. Frank was not so sure about this. Years earlier he had traveled from Europe to Israel for a military mission and was given the same briefing. He had flown with a team on Lufthansa and

Frank was careful to wear clothes that he had bought in German stores as opposed to the PX. He also made a point to speak only German on the plane. When he arrived at Tel Aviv, he was standing in customs apart from the other GIs on his team. There were probably two hundred people standing in line and an Israeli Major in uniform came up to Frank, asked him if he was the American Captain from Germany and Frank said yes. The Israeli officer asked him to point out the other members of his team, one of whom was a Colonel. Frank assumed this was the magic of the Mossad, but he was surprised that they did not know who the Colonel was if he knew a lowly Captain. The Israeli officer said it has nothing to do with intelligence, it was just that Frank looked like an American GI.

Frank did as he was told and flew from Fayetteville of course to Atlanta, then to Miami. At Miami, he boarded the flight bound for Haiti. Frank was travelling on Thanksgiving morning. The plane was totally full. The only persons on the plane who were not Haitian were Frank and three nuns. The nuns obviously didn't get the terrorism brief because they were in their habits. He could have worn his Steeler windbreaker. The flight was somewhat bizarre. Everyone on the flight had tons of carry-on items. The carry-on of choice seemed to be a 5 gallon bucket that you would use for dry wall compound. Everyone had at least one of these buckets. There were also huge rolls of blankets and cages with animals, presumably with chickens in them. As the passengers began to board, it was apparent that the items would not fit in the overhead, but there was no way anyone was giving up their bags to the stewardesses. The reason for that was apparent as soon as we landed. The flight from Miami to Port au Prince was less than an hour, so the stewardesses gave up and the passengers stowed whatever they had wherever they could. The passengers were incredibly friendly and were fascinated that Frank was on the plane with them. Frank told them he was a business man, but since he wasn't in first class they assumed he was a hard worker like them. When the plane landed, it was apparent why no one wanted to give up their bags. The plane landed and the bags were removed from the plane and placed in the middle of an open field. There was no one to check baggage stubs. This was a free for all and Frank also did not check luggage or clearly it could have been stolen. Frank linked up with his soldiers and a driver and a Major from the embassy. Frank had been told that he would stay on a cot in the barracks which was fine, but now the Major said she had made arrangements for him to say in a hotel. Frank ate a Thanksgiving feast with his troops and then linked up with the driver and the Major to go to the hotel. It was just after dusk and already getting dark. The driver explained that the hotel was up in the mountains. As they began the trek up the hill out of Port au Prince, there was a commotion in the road ahead. The driver told Frank to get the gun out of the glove compartment. Frank pulled 9 mm out of the glove compartment, but certainly wasn't sure what he supposed to do with it. This was not covered in the terrorism brief. There was a donkey and a cart jamming up the road. The driver had just enough room to maneuver around the cart jumping the curb and riding on the sidewalk. The people on the sidewalk scattered when they saw the car had no intention of stopping and in fact was now going as fast as possible. The car was a Ford LTD with a trooper engine and was hardened to at least survive small arms attacks. When the driver passed the obstacle, he said that was a favorite tactic of the locals to get the car to stop and then overwhelm the passengers and rob and in some cases beat them. He said he had no intentions of stopping or slowing down and he was glad that he didn't have to run over the donkey, but he definitely would have if he couldn't have got around it. Frank was dropped off at a hotel on top of the hill and given strict orders not to go to the Casino next door that was off limits. Given the Wild West nature of Haiti, it was hard to imagine what could possibly be taking place to get an establishment identified as off limits, but Frank had no interest in going there. The hotel he was staying at was unlike anything he had ever seen. The entire hotel was open air. The weather at the top of the hill was pleasant. It was warm with little or no humidity. This being Haiti, the ratio of employees to guests was about thirty to one. People were falling all over themselves helping Frank with his bag and getting him checked in. His room was bigger than any room he had ever seen. His bed was custom made and appeared to be 10 feet long by 10 feet wide. Frank felt like he was Earnest Hemingway. When he went down to the restaurant it was more of the same. If he even took a sip out of his glass if water someone was there to replace it. The service was incredible. Frank had a great meal. Most of the other guests were French from the Papa Doc days. They had actually gone to Haiti for a vacation. Hard to imagine given what Frank had just seen in Port au Prince that there was a European vacation spot less than five miles away.

Frank's guys did a great job on this deployment and even received a letter of commendation from the Atlantic Command Commander, a four Star Marine Corps General, who was so impressed with their work that he took the time to write a letter that filtered through the XVIII Airborne Corps Commander to Frank's units.

Frank also had to deploy a unit to Bosnia during his tour. A force was sent across the Sava River to bring stability to that region of Europe. Frank's unit was designated to provide maintenance support across the entire area.

At that time at Fort Bragg, units would prepare elaborate rehearsals using scale models. Businesses in Fayetteville could get rich selling scale models of roads, rails, trains, ships, planes, soldiers, mountain ranges. Every unit became proficient at this. This sprang from the rotations at Fort Irwin and were called rock drills because initially commanders would use rocks to display the enemy, obstacles and their own forces so that everyone could orient themselves to the battlefield and understood the commander's intent before they moved out. Some in the Army now will say a ROC drill now is an acronym for rehearsal of Concept, but for Frank it will always be a rock drill. In any event, Fort Bragg had mastered this concept. The only negative was that units would set it up in a gymnasium so there was enough room to emplace all the pieces and then move according to the timeline. A gym also provided plenty of room for unit members to observe and ask questions. The drawback with the gyms was that the layout had to be removed so that the gym could be used or its intended purpose.

Frank really wanted to put on a good Rock drill prior to the Bosnia deployment so he had the idea to use his parachute rigger shed. Frank's unit had the mission to perform parachute maintenance, which on Fort Bragg was big business. He had two companies of parachute riggers that worked all day repairing parachutes, both personnel and cargo parachutes. When Frank arrived the backlog of parachutes was very high. Of course, Frank had never worked around parachutes before and at first just accepted the high backlog as normal, but Frank did like spending time at the rigger shed and observed a lot of standing around. Everyone working in the facility had to be a parachute rigger, which was a very elite specialty that was difficult to obtain. Certainly the soldiers were well motivated. They also had a very high rank structure compared with other units, with a large percentage of noncommissioned officers, warrant officers and lieutenants. Virtually everyone in the unit's leadership structure was a jumpmaster, the most difficult school in the Army to pass. Also, a lot of the unit members had served with the Green Berets. Some had even had the High Altitude Low Opening Parachute badge. Frank had a hard time understanding why there wasn't better production coming out of these units. Once, at a rifle range, Frank was joking with one of the parachute riggers telling him that he must hurry up and qualify so he could get back to the rigger shed to do a half hour of parachute maintenance. The rigger said no problem and in fact he would do eight hours of work in that half hour. Frank asked him to explain what he meant. He said that the rigger units managed the backlog by using man hours prescribed for each job in the maintenance manual. The problem with this was that the man hours in the manual were very inflated. Frank had spent over twenty years as a maintenance manager of all commodities from communication equipment to small arms to tanks and he knew that you could not manage a backlog by using estimated man hours. The best way to manage a backlog was by using a production index. If you fixed more items than came in, then your backlog would come down. If you fixed less items, then your backlog would go up. It was that simple. Other commodities (automotive, generators) were more complex because the backlog typically consisted of items waiting for repair parts, but parts were not applicable for parachutes Also, other commodities required the that the same equipment submitted for repair be returned to the user who was counting the equipment as non-mission capable on readiness reports. The goal was to return all equipment to the owning unit as soon as possible so the unit could train or deploy with all their equipment. Anything down for over 30 days was briefed at high level readiness meetings. Parachutes did not work like that. Unit drew parachutes for jumps but did not own them. At the time the parachutes were not tracked by serial number so there was no need to manage the age of the backlog. The goal should be to fix as many chutes as possible to have them available for the next mission. Frank had them install the Standard Army Maintenance System (SAMS). He directed that the riggers begin fixing more chutes that they took in each week. In fact Frank said he would give them Friday afternoon off if they exceeded certain thresholds, which they did returning the maximum number back for use. Since age was not an issue, the soldiers quickly learned to fix to easy chutes first. Quality Control was not a problem because the inspectors were separate from the maintenance guys. The backlog quickly began to melt away. In fact, it dropped so dramatically that the unit was able to cancel a contract that they had with a women's prison in South Carolina to fix cargo chutes (prisoners could not work on personnel chutes). Some units are very proud of the number of tanks or other weapons systems in their units. Frank's unit had the most sewing machines. There were at least one hundred sewing machines in the two rigger companies. Frank also had a clothing renovation team that repaired uniforms and sleeping bags. His maintenance unit had sewing machines to repair tents and vehicle canvas. It was a small but integral part of the military.

Another achievement that took place during Frank's watch was that he was able to get air conditioning in the rigger shed. The riggers were elite but parachute maintenance was not one of the glamorous aspects of the job. It was hot, tedious and exacting work. Frank decided he would get some air conditioning in the rigger shed. The idea that Frank had was not used, but a lieutenant in the unit took on the challenge. The lieutenant was an aeronautical engineer who graduated from Embry Riddle University and he was like McGyver. He could fix anything. After the first Gulf War, some members of the units brought back air conditioners that they somehow obtained while they were Saudi Arabia (since there were no parachute drops in the Gulf war there was plenty of idle time for the parachute riggers that deployed). In any event they returned with the heat pumps. The lieutenant determined that all they needed was compressors, which he local purchased. There were eight of them. He then coordinated with the post engineers to have them hooked up to the building. The building was huge with a very high ceiling and all were skeptical that this would work. Once turned on, it took about a day to begin to have an effect. It never became as cool as walking down the frozen foods aisle of the grocery store, but it did knock the humidity and most of the heat out of the building and it was actually pleasant to work in even during the summer.

Once the backlog was lowered there was actually some extra space in the huge building that could be used for the rock drill while still being able to maintain parachutes. There would not be a rush to take it down and he could actually have every soldier who was deploying receive the rock drill brief. He also thought he could leave it up at night and invite the spouses in for a briefing. This had never been done before. Like always, Frank had the initial idea, but he paratroopers really ran with it. They brought in some bleachers and cordoned the area off with cargo parachutes. This gave the place a truly operational feel. The COSCOM Commander was so impressed that he invited the Corps Commander down for the briefing. The highlight of the briefing was the intel portion presented by the Brigade S2 who had just transferred in from the Military Intelligence Brigade. He started with intelligence prep of the battlefield using maps to analyze the terrain and weather. Then he did an exhaustive brief on the background of the various ethnic factions. To Frank this was old stuff. Being from Pittsburgh, he had known Croatians his whole life, but to most this was new information. He then showed imagery that he was getting in real time feeds from satellites using his former contacts. The briefing laid out everything from the actual movement from Fort Bragg to the living conditions at the places where they would be staying throughout the deployment. Since they could leave the display in place, the same briefing was given to the spouses that evening. They really appreciated it. They felt a lot better about sending their loved ones into harm's way, knowing that so much professionalism had gone into the preparation. Deploying to semi hot combat zones was fairly new to the volunteer Army. Frank expected to have a lot of trouble with the stay behind personnel, but that was far from the case. In fact the opposite was true. Frank had heard that one of the spouses had a tree fall on her roof. She was actually handicapped and Frank saw her in the parking lot and asked her how she was doing. She was very hesitant to tell Frank anything. Finally she told Frank that there was a rumor going around that if you complained, Frank would bring the spouse back from deployment and replace him or her with someone else. Frank had no idea where this was coming from, so he gathered all of the spouses and told them that redeploying someone was the last thing he would do. Every soldier who had deployed was essential and no one was coming back early. He still had a thousand soldiers at Fort Bragg with him and they could handle any emergency that might arise. After the briefing, one of the spouses came up to Frank and told him that while the deployment was hard due to the separa-tion, the family was finally getting on its feet financially. The com-bat pay, separation pay and tax free income, combined with other benefits, allowed families to move beyond living from paycheck to paycheck. It was the reason why there were no complaints. This was another lesson that Frank learned about combat. Soldiers and their spouses will endure almost anything if they feel they are being well led, well equipped and fairly compensated.

The unit that deployed was well led and had a Puerto Rican commander who was a superb leader. He was a jumpmaster and incredibly physically fit. Since he was from Puerto Rico, Frank correctly assumed that he idolized Roberto Clemente and Frank brought him back a picture of the "great one" after one of his trips to Pittsburgh, which the he took with him and displayed prominently. By a quirk of fate, the unit had a great softball team and the Colonel they worked for in Tazar, Hungary, was also a softball fan. It was a match made in heaven.

Once again Frank made arrangements to visit his troops on the next Thanksgiving. This time he went with the COSCOM com-mander, a one star general. Frank had gone with him on several previous visits. The trips always involved staying in Budapest on the front end and back end of the trip. Budapest is a beautiful city and in fact reminded Frank somewhat of Pittsburgh due to the hills rising up from the river, although not many people mistake the Monongahela for the Danube. When they would touch down in Budapest, they would be met by a State Department rep. The rep would organize an elaborate dinner for the general and his party. The restaurant was in the basement of an old hotel. It had been in business since the middle ages. It had wooden beams in the ceilings and a beautiful wooden floor. When the team of Americans went for the first time, they were typical American, complaining about a delay between the serving of the soup and the next course, which was a salad. The state department rep told them that this was not McDonalds. This meal was an event and they would be there all night. It was not fast food. He encouraged the team to get some wine, which they did, and they started to relax. The meal did last all night and it was superb. They were entertained by gypsies' dancing and playing the violin throughout the evening. It was a great experience. They went to Tazar, Hungary the next day and had to eat two Thanksgiving meals. One at Tazar and one at Slovinsky Brod. Fortunately all were airborne and would run the meals off. The team traveled in convoys that required them to don helmets, flak vests and to draw weapons. At one point in the trip they were transported on a host nation Army helicopter, which was a Vietnam era Huey or UH1 that had long since vanished from the Army inventory. The general was in the copilot seat and could not help but stare at the master caution light that was on for the entire trip. Little things like gages did not seem to concern the pilot. Fortunately there was no incident because they traveled over some of the most rugged terrain in the world. There would be no way anyone could get to the team on foot or vehicle if they went down

The team returned to a Corps level exercise. The exercise was conducted on Fort Bragg and was to include the 2 brigades from the 10th Mountain as the OPFOR against the 82d Airborne, the Marines from Camp Lejeune and the XVIII Airborne Corps.

Two days before the exercise was to begin, Frank's boss called and told him there would been change of plans to he exercise. The 10th Mountain was snowed in and only the Brigade Commander, his staff and one Infantry battalion could deploy to Fort Bragg. They needed a large unit to serve as an additional maneuver unit for the OPF0R and Frank's unit was nominated. Frank figured it would be a good change of pace for his guys and his Command Sergeant Major, who had spent time supporting the Special Forces really embraced the mission. The CSM used several mobile platoons as decoys to fool the reconnaissance assets flying overhead. He made sure our unit was dug in, conducted patrols and enforced noise and light discipline. He even managed to capture a long range reconnaissance patrol member who parachuted in and essentially landed on his tent. When the Recon guy saw the size of the unit and all the equipment, he couldn't believe was dropped right on top of the unit. The Brigade Commander from Fort Drum also ran a tight ship. He had radio updates and back briefs four times a day. When he issued an order he wanted it read back to him verbatim. When he visited Frank's unit, he was impressed with the tactics and was very impressed with the Captain serving as the Battalion S-3 who escorted him around the perimeter. An Infantry Battalion would never have a Captain as the S-3. The Brigade Commander was so impressed that he mentioned it to the Corps Commander at the end of the exercise, resulting in the Corps Commander writing a note to the COSCOM Commander saying how impressed he was with the logistics battalion that served as the OPFOR. Also while the Brigade Commander was there he was offered some hard boiled eggs by the Mess Sergeant. The exercise was began with the typical A C A meaning two hot meals with a C Ration for lunch. Once the maneuver phase of the exercise started the rations would be only Cs. The mess sergeant had strong ties to the battalion. Even in the time of consolidated dining facilities the Mess Sergeant and his cooks were an integral part of the battalion. On jumps he would show up on the drop zone with hot coffee and soup. No one requested it, probably no one approved it, but he was always there. For this exercise he saved some cake mix and hard boiled eggs and other treats to augment the C rations. He offered two hard boiled eggs to the brigade commander. It was a fairly cold morning and the brigade commander, after eating only C rations for several days, thought the eggs were like a four course meal.

Frank's unit had been through the EXEVAL, the lives fires, a JRTC rotation during his command tour as well as deployments to Haiti and Bosnia and provided support to victims of Hurricane Fran in two years' which was fairly typical OPTEMPO for Fort Bragg for logistics units.

Harley

Track

Club Football

Riding in California

Alps

Schweinfurt Germany

Airborne

Fort Bragg Change of Command

Iraq

C17 Flight to Afghanistan

Bagram, Afghanistan

Container Handler

Donor and Recipient Marking 5 Years

Walking Down the Aisle

Chapter 10
The Battalion Commander and the National Training Center

Frank had a developmental assignment as an instructor at the Ordnance Center and School. Almost as soon as he arrived he was selected to go to observe a rotation at the National Training Center. Frank jumped at the chance as his last assignment in Germany was more administrative than tactical. Upon his arrival he was initially paired with a Lieutenant Colonel who had spent four years stationed at the National Training Center. His first two years were spent as an observer/controller. This was followed by his selection to command a battalion in the 11th Armored Calvary regiment. This was the famed Black Horse Regiment that was stationed in the Fulda Gap during the Cold War. It was probably the most famous regiment in the Army and had produced its share of Generals. At Fort Irwin the unit served as the opposing forces. It was lighter and more nimble than the American Forces that rotated through the training center. They used converted Sheridan tanks that were a nightmare to maintain but they were fast and could maneuver in difficult, tight terrain. That suited the battalion commander just fine. At West Point, He played on the sprint football team. In fact that was one of the reasons he attended West Point. Not many schools had a sprint football team. Sprint football was played by the service academies and some Ivy League schools. Players had to be under 172 lbs. to play. He loved playing football in high school but at 165 lbs. he did not think that playing in college would be an option. He played defensive back for his small high school but at West Pont he played guard on the sprint football team. The teams in the league empathized speed and leverage, not power and mass. There was not enough sprint football teams to fill out an entire schedule so that the teams would often play junior colleges or a junior varsity team from a local college. The battalion commander loved these games. Often as a guard he would be lining up with a 250 lbs. opponent three inches from him on the line. But the game was called sprint football, not lightweight football or stand around and watch what was happening football. The plays involved misdirection, pulling linemen, sweeps, short passes and anything that could get the opponent moving in the wrong direction of only for a split second. The commander learned quickly that the only way to excel was to always be moving at breakneck speed. If you stopped and looked around a brutal hit was your reward. These were the same tactics used by the OPFOR. Of course, they knew the terrain giving them the ultimate home field advantage. They also went to the field for three weeks every month. No unit in any Army had ever been as tactically proficient or as knowledgeable about field craft as the 11th ACR. During one rotation, engineers on the rotating brigade spent an entire day emplacing an obstacle between two cliffs. This was to slow and fix the OPFOR so they could be decimated with artillery and airpower. The battalion commander's scouts had reported the obstacle when the battalion's formation was about 5 kilometers out. The scouts also said if the OPFOR got up enough speed they could bypass the obstacle. The battalion commander never wanted to slow down much less stop he took the information and upon arriving at the obstacle sent the first Sheridan to left of the obstacle. This meant the Sheridan had to get up enough speed to use centrifugal force to o stay on the side of the cliff. All remaining Sheridans followed suit. The obstacle was by passed with less than a thirty second delay, allowing the OPFOR to wreak havoc on the advance guard of the rotating unit, then quickly fade way before the main body of the rotation force arrived. The soldiers stationed at the NTC played an unsung role during the Cold War was the soldiers assigned to the National Training Center at Fort Irwin, California, in the heart of the Mohave Desert. The Army needed a world class training facility with enough land to wage tank battles at the brigade level. The training area was established in the 1980s as part of the Reagan buildup, although incredibly it was Jimmy Carter who first started to organize a rapid deployment force with the mission to respond to threats in the Mideast. This of course proved to be prophetic. The Army placed world class, cutting edge training equipment at Fort Irwin. Vehicles and soldiers were outfitted with the Multiple Laser Engagement System. For the first time, soldiers and leaders could safely determine if their tactics were effective. All that needed to be done was to man the training area. This involved assigning the equivalent of a brigade to serve as a professional, thinking enemy. They also sent very successful officers and noncommissioned officers for three year assignments to serve as leader trainers. In effect, the Army was sending several thousand soldiers to the middle of the desert. There was little infrastructure on the base; not much in the way of schools or family housing, but that changed quickly. On top of that, the soldiers were told that the intent was to push an Army brigade through the training facility at a rate of one per month. The brigade would undergo a three week force on force exercise. That meant that the soldiers assigned to Fort Irwin would spend three weeks of every month in the desert for three years. Even if there was a break in the exercise action, it was almost impossible to return to the post or to the town of Barstow. The exercise was conducted over an hour drive from the main post and the town of Barstow, where some soldiers lived, was over an hour from the main post. On top of that, the road from the main post to the town of Barstow was one of the most dangerous in America. Soldiers not used to the wide open spaces in the desert had a difficult time driving, and the main danger was the hypnotic effect of driving on a road where you could literally see for miles ahead. There was nothing close to concentrate on. The road has dozens of crosses marking locations where soldiers' had lost control and crashed. Of course if soldiers were exhausted from operating in the desert, this only added to the danger. It was not long before the Army restricted travelling during the exercise period. Thus, three weeks of every month were spent in the desert.

Frank spent the second half of the rotation with one of the Observer Controllers. Since most of the leader trainers had their own HMMWVs to conduct the evaluations and keep up with the Armor units they were evaluating, they tricked them out with grills, radios, and sleeping quarters. Not all of the permanently stationed soldiers were pleased to have an outsider join their midst, especially the Infantry trainers. They had the nickname of the Scorpions and were a tough group of guys. Frank was linked up with a lieutenant who was getting out of the Army and was assigned to evaluate logistics. These exercises were not really designed to stress logistics (other than maintenance). These exercises were designed to test performance in combat. The lieutenant was tasked to go to each motor pool in the morning and then report back to his superiors. He was essentially done at lunchtime. Frank and the lieutenant drove to a place in the desert where the infantry leader trainers gathered every day. As they turned the bend, Frank could not believe what he was seeing. There were about forty guys performing various activities in various stages of undress. Some of the guys were lifting weights. Some were playing basketball. Others were eating lunch. There was a shower set up on the site. The lieutenant explained that as the guys did various activities, it was so hot you could only spend about 10 minutes working out before you would get so hot that you needed a shower. It did not make sense to constantly put clothes on. Frank quickly got something to eat and asked the lieutenant what his plans were for the afternoon. Frank definitely didn't want to stay with the half-naked infantrymen. The lieutenant said he usually drove into the mountains and looked for gold. Frank thought that sounded better than staying where he was. The lieutenant took off in the HMMWV. The lieutenant treated his HMMWV like it was his own personal dune buggy. He almost never took a road. Roads had speed limits and even deep in the desert, MPs were patrolling and handing out tickets. The lieutenant immediately headed into the mountains. His specialty was cresting hills at full speed getting all four wheels off the ground. He also loved driving sideways on the mountains using speed and momentum to keep from tipping over. Frank mentioned to the lieutenant that he had fielded (essentially provided training) to units in Germany that were getting the new vehicles and one of the things that they would tell the troops is that you could not roll a HMMWV due to the wide base. The lieutenant replied that was not correct and that they rolled them all the time at Fort Irwin. Frank immediately ordered him to slow down. While everyone had tricked out their HMMWVs, his was unique. His was outfitted with picks, shovels and strainers. Every few miles he would stop and get out and start working the hillside with his pick. He explained that he looked for quartz veins. Then he would start picking away at the quartz. He would spend about twenty minutes doing this and if he didn't find anything he would go back to the HMMWV and speed to the next site.

Frank linked up with the rest of the team in a hotel in Barstow to write a report. Three weeks in the desert was quite enough. It was almost unbelievable that soldiers did that for three year tours. One guy Frank met had extended for another year. He had actually participated in 46 rotations. These guys were the true heroes of the cold war. It was a reason the Army transformed from an almost dysfunctional organization of the seventies to the professional force that routed Iraq in 11 days during the 1st Gulf War. Most of the officers had gone thru multiple rotations at Fort Irwin and were well prepared. Also, units were the beneficiaries of getting soldiers assigned who were part of the OPFOR at Fort Irwin. These soldiers became the best trained force in the world and could infuse an aggressive attitude into any unit.

Chapter 11

Leadership

Frank went to a small college in Pennsylvania. There was no ROTC and he certainly did not envision a military career. He never took a leadership course, but attending that small college offered plenty of opportunity for hands on leadership training. The college had a Club Football team. That meant that they played normal intercollegiate football, but the students themselves raised the money to fund the program. Frank went out for the team even though he did not play football in high school. The team was an eclectic mix of former high school players, townies who wanted to extend their glory days, Vietnam veterans, late bloomers who didn't play in high school (Frank was in this category) and one or two actual great football players. The team was also on the cutting edge of using basketball players on the football team. The small college attracted quite a few really great high school basketball players that had the dream of walking on and earning a basketball scholarship, but the numbers were against them. The college would give four or five scholarships per year so some of these walk-ons would make the JV team but very rarely did a walk-on play for the varsity. But these were guys who were big, fast, coordinated and competitive, were welcomed by the football team with open arms. The defensive end who played opposite Frank was a 6'4 high school basketball star from New Jersey who played on the college JV basketball team for two years. Incredibly, in his first game, he intercepted a lazy screen pass and ran it back for a touchdown. The team also had a wide receiver that played basketball. He couldn't block, couldn't hit a sled and actually could not even get into a three point stance, but if you threw a football anywhere near him he would catch it. He was especially effective on curls and button hooks where he would box out the defender and go up and grab the ball. But the number one convert actually had come to the college on a basketball scholarship. He was 6' 7" and weighed over 325 lbs. He played for a small Catholic high school in Pittsburgh and dominated for two reasons: he played in small gyms that were more suited for elementary schools so he didn't really need to run and he also almost never played against anyone who could really leap, so he didn't have to worry about anyone out jumping him. When he got to college it was quickly apparent that he could not get up and down the court. Also, the other scholarship guys on the team were not as impacted by his wide body blocking them out. Several could go up from behind him and grab rebounds, because he could not get more than one or two inches off the ground. During his junior year, he was dropped from the basketball team and he came out for football. Unlike the other basketball players who used their athleticism to compete, he had a hard time with the transition. The coach wanted to use him at defensive tackle and all he wanted him to do was lie down and plug two or three holes with his mass. He could not break the habit if standing up when the ball was snapped and looking around. During one routine play at practice, he stood up, and the offensive guard, who was 5' 8" and 155 lbs., put his shoulder pads into the basketball convert's thighs and drove him 20 yards off the ball. The play ended at the line of scrimmage, but the coach noticed he was pushed back over twenty yards. He stopped practice to ask how that could have happened and begged him just to fall down. Since he was listed at

6'7" and 325 lbs., he looked so good in the program that the Dallas Cowboys invited him to try out on size alone. He did not last long but he was able to integrate that the Dallas Cowboys asked him to try out into his conversations. He was already a smooth talker and he would pick out the smallest girl at a party or dance and basically challenge her by saying that she couldn't handle a big man like him and since he could add the Dallas Cowboy tryout to his lines, he got a lot of dates from 4 ft. 11 inch 95 lb. girls.

He wasn't the only unique character. One guy asked the coach if he could try out for the team as a holder on the field goals and extra points. The coach said sure he could come out but did not mention that we never kicked field goals and after our quarterback got hurt, we didn't score many touchdowns. He also didn't mention that on most days the team barely had 22 able bodies at practice to piece together a scrimmage. On his first day practice, the team lined up for a scrimmage after the warm ups. The team was short an offensive guard so the coach told the 5ft 10" 145 lb. newcomer to go in and play guard. He knew better than to say he just signed up to be the holder, so he told the coach he didn't know the plays. The coach said that was not a problem. Just get in the way of the guy in front of you. That happened to be one of our biggest and best defenders. He was from the storied DeMatha high program out of D.C. and he actually played basketball for them. The college gave him a full ride one because he was a good student and they assumed he would contribute on the basketball team. He really was not a basketball player and didn't even try out for the team. He was a good football player, however, tailor made for the defensive line. He had huge forearms and calves and an extra-large backside that gave him a low center of gravity despite being 6 foot 3. He teed off on the newcomer on the first play, smacking his rather poor fitting helmet with one of his forearms. That one play ended our full time kick holder's football career.

The coach during Frank's first year had gone to the same college when they had an actual team not a club team and he was a small college All American. He was way better than anyone on the current team even though he was approaching 40. There was nothing he couldn't do on a football field. He was a superb punter and the team would watch him kick beautiful spirals into the coffin corner a term that is no longer in use. During one pre practice punting exhibition, he put ten punts inside the two yard line. Punters don't even try to do that now. Then again, punters now aren't typically All American running backs. His favorite pastime at practice was to show the running back how to hit the hole. Usually two or three plays into the scrimmage he would tell the running back to stand back and watch how it should be done. Then he would yell go live and run the play. The team loved the coach and wouldn't try to tackle him, which really got his blood boiling. He would run it again, but no one would hit him. Actually even if the defenders wanted to tackle him, it was not certain that it could be done. He was so fast and so quick that he would have been hard to touch him, let alone tackle him. Regrettably, the coach left after Frank's sophomore year and the team went through a coach a year after that.

During Frank's first year the team was very good. The captains were the quarterback and the tight end. The tight end was a tough kid from Aliquippa who modeled his leadership style after Mike Ditka, another tight end from Aliquippa. The team was playing a game in Ohio and was down by six at the half. The team moped into the locker room. The captain entered last and he told the coaches to stay out of the room. The Captain slammed the door shut then smashed his helmet on top of a locker. He had everyone's attention. He started by saying that everyone who was thinking about partying that night better get that idea out of his mind right now. Frank thought he was looking right into his soul. It was doubtful Frank would play and he was in fact, thinking about getting a case of beer and partying that night. From the sheepish looks on the faces of the other players, it looked like he was not the only one. The captain said that no one was leaving if we didn't win the game. He said he would personally lead a four hour full contact practice session immediately after the game. He accentuated that by getting up in the face of every player and looked him in the eye and asked if he had made himself clear. The second half was not even close and the team returned with a victory

The kicker was another strange case. In those days, most teams still kicked using the Lou Groza toe punch method. The team's best player, Hoagie, was the center and he had been offered over one hundred scholarships coming out of high school. He had tree trunks for legs and while not fast, he was incredibly quick and he had a mean streak. Because he was built with a barrel chest his proportions made it seem like he wasn't quite as tall as the six foot four inches he actually was. He transferred into the small college literally a man among boys (almost all the schools in the league had one or two division 1 caliber players that for some reason ended up playing for a local small college), In fact, on the first day that Hoagie showed up for practice one of the players behind Frank was counting the players in line and the players in the other line then asked to switch with Frank. When Frank asked why, he said he had gone to high school with Hoagie and he did not want to go against him in an Oklahoma drill. While Frank was skeptical, he also did not want to be the guinea pig. They rushed a freshmen to the front of the line to go against Hoagie and, as predicted, Hoagie flattened him. Hoagie could boom a kickoff into or near the end zone and could certainly kick an extra point, but was not precise enough for field goals. Every day when the team would take the field, one of the students would be on the field booming kicking soccer style field goals. The team begged him to come out and he reluctantly agreed after the first game. The team was healthy at this point and we had high hopes for the season. A kicker who could make forty yard field goals would be a great asset.

The team played their first game in downtown Pittsburgh on a dirt and rock strewn city league field. The team did not have the kicker but easily defeated a large commuter school, even though they had an enrollment of about 20,000 students to draw from. Several minutes prior to game time, a Pittsburgh taxi cab pulled up and a rather large black men got out of the cab, pulled a helmet, shoulder pads and uniform out of the trunk, ran into the locker room came out and was the starting outside linebacker. Several things of note happened that day. The defensive end (a basketball player originally) opposite Frank intercepted a pass, and him and Frank being the only two moving toward the goal when the play began, waltzed together into the end zone. It was also the game that Frank's friend broke his collar bone. His friend was an excellent wrestler and a tough kid from New Kensington, Pa. He was a good athlete, but had never played organized football. He came out for the team one week before the first game. Driving to the game on the bus, Frank and the others were saying that they were nervous. Frank's friend said he was not nervous because there was no way he was going to play. Frank was not so sure. Although he was short and he wrestled at 132, he was tough, fearless and he had a commodity that was in short supply on the team: he had speed. Shortly before the end of the first half, he was sent in to play defensive back. On his first play, Frank's team intercepted he ball and Frank's friend immediately set out to block the offensive tackle from during the return. The converted wrestler, weighing in at 135 pounds, running at full speed with limited technique, met 260 pounds of offensive tackle and the result was a broken collar bone. Frank stayed with him throughout the halftime as his uniform had to be cut off. His bone was protruding through the skin. That not only ended his football career but also his wrestling career. Frank felt bad for his friend and was determined to motivate his teammates to extract revenge in the second half. The team ended up winning easily.

The next week, the kicker came out for the team. The team members were all pleased and they treated him gently. He was booming kicks in practice, but he never kicked against a defense. The next game was a home game against another in state college. The home team quickly went up 18 to nothing. Why 18. The college scored three touchdowns but the new kicker was unable to make an extra point in three tries. After the first touchdown, the coach sent the kicker in and when he saw an angry defense lined up against him, he lost all form and barely got a foot on the ball. The ball dribbled off to the left side of the line and never even cleared the line. The coach figured it was just nerves. The next PAT was even worse. He was leaning back so far he barely made contact with the ball. The third attempt produced similar results, but the team was playing well and confident of victory. Then early in the third quarter the quarterback stepped in a hole while he was being hit and his lower leg snapped. To say the team did not have a backup was an understatement. There was no backup. No one else even knew the plays. The team went three and out for the rest of the game and ended up losing 20 to 18. The team could have blamed the loss on the injury to the quarterback or the fact that we had no backup. In fact, Frank missed a tackle on a flea flicker that resulted in a touchdown. But everyone on the team placed the blame on the kicker. On Monday, when the team showed up for practice all the players were taking turns toe punching extra points. When the coach came out, he said we were going to start practice by kicking extra points. He also said we would be going live which the team usually did not do on Mondays. The team lined up on both sides of the ball and Hoagie our superstar center snapped the ball back. The hold was good and the line was holding their blocks but of course there was some pressure up the middle and the ends were coming around getting ready to dive for the ball. This was enough to make the kicker transfer his weight to his back foot and of course he picked his head up to see what was coming at him. He struck the ball about midway up and he sent a screaming line drive right into Hoagie's backside. That was enough for Hoagie. He turned and went after the kicker. No one made a quick move to stop him, not even the coach. The team technically didn't cut anyone but that was the way of team telling the kicker he was no longer welcome.

Frank managed to stay uninjured throughout the season. Frank did take a vicious hit during the next game. That game was instrumental for a few reasons. First, Frank was taking a course in Victorian Literature. He was English major and he had to take a set number of seminars. At the small college, that meant being in a class with six or seven other English majors and the department head, who of course had a PhD. There was nowhere to hide in those classes. The professor made it clear that class participation was 50% of the grade and all were supposed to come to class prepared. At the end of every practice, the team had to jog a mile around the fields. Frank would sprint this. He would also run up the huge hill to the gym. Some people on the team thought Frank was just trying to impress the coach but he was actually getting to the gym quickly so he could take a shower and be dressed before the big linemen came into the locker room and filled it up. This also had the added advantage of getting Frank to the dining facility first. The food was prepared by German nuns and most of the food was grown on the college farm. Frank would eat till he was ready to burst then he would go to his room where his roommate would have a quart of beer waiting for him. Frank would start drinking the beer and try to get though the Victorian Literature homework which typically had a requirement to read a hundred page poem that didn't rhyme and was about death. Frank just couldn't get through them. He was unable to participate in class.

During the Friday class before the game, the professor told everyone in the class that they should go watch the football game. He was an alumnus of the team they were playing, but now his allegiance was to the college where he taught. One of Frank's classmates told the professor that Frank played on the football team. Frank confirmed this and told the professor that his number was 80 and that he played defensive end. During the game, the other team threw swing pass to the opposite end of where Frank played. The pass fell harmlessly incomplete. Frank saw this and essentially stopped but the other teams fullback did not. The fullback was a typical fullback, tough, loved to hit and had the traditional bowling ball build, short, stocky and powerful. He didn't see the pass drop, there was no whistle and he didn't stop. He coiled up and unleashed a brutal hit on Frank. He smashed Frank's jaw and drove his helmet up into Franks head. Frank fell in a heap. Almost on autopilot, Frank got up and played the next play which was a punt. On the sidelines, Frank was essentially knocked out. His roommate, who, like all the students, was sitting on the hill that rose up from the field. The school used to play their games in a downtown high school stadium and that was a big money loser. Also, very few of the students would come to the game. A business student, who basically raised money to keep the team afloat, had the idea to move the games on campus. The campus had great fields, but it had no seating. The business student rented some bleachers and a flatbed truck for the announcer, who was also a student and who brought his own stereo with a microphone. He charged the townies and the parents a nominal fee to sit in the bleachers but the students could spill out of the dorms and sit on the hill and watch the game for free. All the students came and quickly formed a pep band that played on the hillside. The announcer was a good friend of Frank's and if he couldn't see who made the tackle he would say tackle made by Frank. One game Frank was credited with making twenty tackles, some made while he was on the sideline. Playing on campus led to a rather informal separation between the fans and the players. In fact there was no separation. Frank's roommate saw that Frank had been lit up and walked down to the sideline to see if Frank was ok. Frank's roommate took him aside, got him some water and basically talked to him till his brain become unclouded. Fortunately the offense made a few first downs and Frank was ok and able to go back into the game.

After the game, Frank's professor came up to him and introduced his wife and kids. The professor even mentioned what a great game Frank played during Monday's class, which wasn't technically true, but he did get his name called on the loudspeaker because his friend was announcing the game. All of this did not have an effect on his grade however. At the end of the semester the professor told Frank that he would get a C even though his papers and test scores were solid Bs. Bottom line: Frank did not participate in class and that was 50% of the grade. Football was no excuse. There are a lot of advantages to being at a small college, but when you are in a seminar with less than 10 people you cannot fake your way through and he was given a C for the course. One of only two Cs he received in college.

Frank did have a glory game during his senior year. The college travelled to Buffalo late in the season. The college was always traveling to Buffalo. The game was played in November and it was already getting cold. Frank put a black sweatshirt under his shoulder pads and it really made them fit good. The team went out for warm-ups and Frank really felt great. The team went back in the locker room and the coach said he wanted to have the team select two captains. Their best player, Hoagie, did not come on the trip because he was taking law boards. Frank was standing off to the side getting his thigh wrapped when the coach asked the team to vote on two captains. Frank said that Mike should be one captain and there was no need to vote. When the team went out on the field, the coach said Mike and Frank go out for the coin toss. Frank was so surprised that he asked the coach if he really meant him. The coach said he only heard two names Frank and Mike. Frank ended up being the only defensive player who was a captain because Mike got hurt right away. The opposing college had a superstar running back. Like Frank's team, who had Hoagie, they had a player who was clearly division 1 talent but for some reason ended up in club football. During the first series of plays the running back came around Frank's end and he was tackled after a short gain. They punted and Frank came off the field. The Dean of Students was attending the game and he walked up to Frank and told him that he was bleeding. Frank looked down at his left arm and it was covered in blood. The Dean was standing on the sideline and he told Frank that he must have a cut on his arm. There was so much blood it was dripping onto his thigh pad. Frank went over to the water bucket and washed the blood off his arm and he was surprised to find that there was no cut on his arm. It obviously wasn't his blood. Frank was also surprised that the superstar running back did not play again in the first half. With him missing, the game became a three and out defensive struggle. Frank was having a good game and he enjoyed calling the defensive signals and having the head referee consult him on the penalties. At the beginning of the second half the superstar was back in the backfield. He had a butterfly bandage across his nose. After the game, Frank was told that in that first series when Frank thought he made a routine tackle, what actually happened was Frank's blade thin forearm slipped between the facemask and the helmet with enough force to break his nose and give him a concussion. It was by far Frank's best game and he really enjoyed the role of Captain, making all the defensive calls and conferring with the refs on penalties.

Frank did not realize it at the time but playing football in college totally shaped the rest of his life. Frank, like several players on the team, did not play football in high school. He tried out as a freshman in high school and was too skinny and too slow and was cut. He then put all his effort into making the basketball team as a sophomore. He ended up being cut from that as well. The numbers at his high school worked against him. There were 810 students in the graduating class. Too many guys who developed a lot quicker than normal. Frank went out for cross country and track and by Class AAAA WPIAL standards he wasn't very good at that either, but it did allow him to make a good group of friends and it got him used to persevering through hard races and workouts. At least no one got cut from those teams.

Frank arrived at the small college at the beginning of his sophomore year after transferring and figured being on the Club football team would be a good way to make friends. It was. But Frank did not realize that for the rest of his life he could tell bosses and co-workers that he played football in college. Then he usually left the rest to the imagination of who he was talking to. Most assumed if you played football in college at any level that you must have been a great high school football player. They also assumed that Saturday games were on television with big crowds and a big band playing at halftime. He could even mention that they played in Three Rivers Stadium, which was true. The stadium of course had artificial turf and the team was told they would be provided soccer style shoes. They were not. Frank had a pair of high top Chuck Taylor Converse tennis shoes in his gym bag and they worked just fine. It was hard playing in the stadium however. Since it was used for Pirate baseball and Steeler football, there were huge zippers in the field to remove the turf for the bases and pitcher's mound. There was also a tilt to the field. The stadium was not oval so the football field was crossways within the stadium. Frank never felt like he knew where he was in relation to the sideline. Also, playing in front of less than 500 hundred people in a stadium that holds 55,000 was disorienting. In fact there would have been less than five hundred but Frank's dad was coaching his brother's pee wee football team and brought the entire team to the game. Playing at Three Rivers Stadium would add to the perception that Frank played big time football case, but Frank tried to neither dissuade nor encourage what they thought. Frank always recommends a small college to anyone that attended a mega high school and had a hard time even participating in sports or drama or extracurricular activities. The small college experience also added immeasurably to his confidence. His track and cross country background allowed him to excel during Army training runs and tests and he even ran the 800 at the US Army Europe championships. He was also able to participate in unit level flag football, basketball and softball teams, which gave him some measure of street cred with the enlisted guys after he became an officer.

Chapter 12
Steel

The reason Frank joined the military was tied directly to the job he had after he graduated from college. Frank spent the year after he graduated from college working at United States Steel Homestead Works. He shared an apartment with a college friend. Somehow they both got jobs at the same steel plant. Frank's mom had to pull strings to get Frank hired and Frank's roommate's father was an executive at US Steel, but it was still amazing that they both were hired by the same plant an placed on the same shift. Steel companies in Pittsburgh were unrivalled in the mid-seventies. They operated 24 hours per day seven days per week. It was hot, dirty, dangerous work. It paid well. Of course everyone was in the United Steelworkers Union. The first day of work at a steel mill was a unique experience. You were given fire retardant suit, metatarsals to place over your boots and glasses that allowed you to look at molten steel without hurting your eyes. There was no welcome committee, no in brief, no cup of coffee. You were expected to go right to work. For Frank that meant being assigned a third helper. Walking through the mill on the first day, Frank felt like he was involved in a post-apocalyptic movie. Everything in the mill was in motion and on fire. Most of the mill was open air. Frank worked in an open hearth mill. The open hearth was the second link the steel chain. The first link was the coke works. For United States Steel, that mill was in Clairton (Deer Hunter fame). That is where raw materials were fed into a furnace. The process gave off a sulfuric smell that smelled like rotten eggs. The molten metal then was transported down the Monongahela River to Homestead. The Homestead mill employed almost thirty thousand people. People would be bused in from as far as Uniontown. They were good jobs with good pay and benefits. You could have a good life, buy a home, and raise a family on the pay. The mill basically consisted of two levels. The top level consisted of 11 furnaces. One was always down for maintenance. A rail line ran thru the upper level and the rail cars were filled with scrap metal and junk cars. This scrap metal was fed into the front of the furnace. The open hearth furnace is built on steel plates which are supported by I beams. The capacity of the furnace is about 60 tons of metal. There were charging doors on the front and a tapping hole on the opposite back side of the furnace. There are two ports on each end of the furnace which force air and gas into the furnace, where they mix and the gas burns. A supply of natural gas from the gas main passes through a conduit through highly heated brick works that serves as the gas regenerator. Air drawn from the atmosphere enters the furnace, passes through the brick work. Both the gas and the air are highly heated by passing through the brick work of the respective regenerator. At intervals of about thirty minutes the process is reversed, causing a reversal of the path that forces gas to enter the furnace. This system makes possible the absorption of heat which the open hearth process requires. The furnace is charged with pig iron, limestone and steel scrap. The purpose of this operation is to remove the silicon, manganese, carbon, phosphorus and sulfur from the charge. The doors are tightly closed after charging and the heat is regulated to melt the whole charge gradually. As the charge becomes more and more fluid, the iron and scrap are mixed, distributing the impurities evenly throughout the concoction. The lime and iron oxide float to the surface of the molten iron and mixes with the slag which has begun to firm from the oxidized silicon and manganese and from the earthy matter of the charge. The slag spreads out evenly over the iron protecting it from the oxidizing action of the flame. As the silicon and manganese decrease in the metal, the oxidation of carbon increases causing the charge to boil due to the formation and escape of carbon. The melting foreman watches the progress of the operation through peep holes in the furnace doors, protecting his eyes with dark colored glasses that flip in front of the safety glasses. The melting foreman has to regulate the removal of carbon and phosphorus. If the carbon is burning too fast it is necessary to pig up the charge by adding solid pig to increase the carbon and chill the bath. If the phosphorus is going too fast as compared to the carbon, the consumption of carbon can be hastened by adding iron to supply oxygen to consume the carbon. It is essential that an excess of iron oxide should not be added toward the end of the process as an undue amount of iron at the end of the process distributes itself throughout the steel greatly impairing the quality. This is a process that relies highly on experience. Of course, some of the foremen were engineers; but nothing in school could prepare a person to know when to add carbon and how much to add. . Most of the melting foremen had worked their way up through the ranks from first helper to melting foremen. These men had years of experience working with steel and were the reason why these mills were without peer existed for so long, because it used a simple process to create even specialty steel.

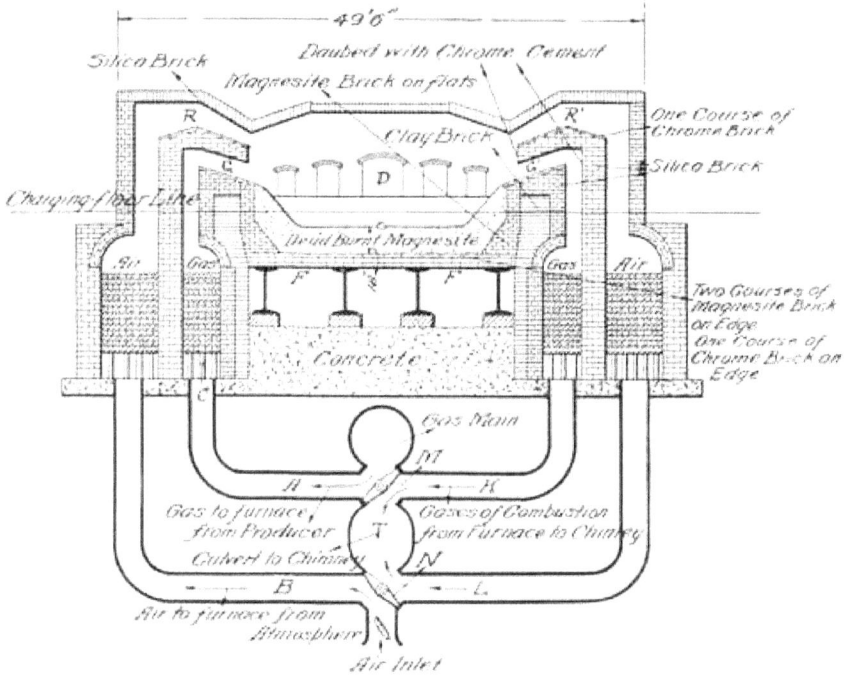

diagram[1]

The back end of the furnace was the scene most people see when a steel mill is shown on TV. There is a small plug in the back of the furnace. Then there is a cement spout that is connected to the furnace and makes a trough that feeds into a ladle. In this open hearth the ladle was over thirty feet high with a thirty foot circumference. Frank's job was the third helper. The first helper was essentially a supervisor who kept the furnace running. The second helper worked with a welding torch and a tanker bar and he connected the spout to the furnace. He spent most of his time behind the furnace. It was definitely the most dangerous job in the mill. The melting foreman's (a bona fide supervisor with a white hard hat) job was to create the

---

1   An Elementary Outline of Mechanical Processes, G. w. Danforth Publisher Phillip Alger PG 95

exact type of steel needed for the end product. This means that the molten steel had to be the correct carbon level when it was tapped (done). The melting foreman could have carbon added to the steel but he could not have it taken away. The process for a batch of steel typically took one shift or eight hours. As the steel was close to being ready, samples were taken by the first helper and sent to a lab. Based on the lab results the melting foreman would then direct when the steel or heat was tapped. At this time the second helper was working feverishly on the back of the furnace unplugging the hole in the back. He then threw a blasting cap that was attached to a long tube through the hole into the furnace. At that time, every siren and alarm in the mill was blaring. It was already an incredibly loud operation and the alarms just added to the sense of impending doom and disaster. The alarm would blare until there was an explosion. Then the molten steel would come pouring out through the hole in the back of the furnace and through the spout and into the ladle. Again samples were being taken. At this time, the melting foreman would direct that carbon be added to the steel. This was the job of the third helper. If the melting foreman was good, you would have to add only three or four 100 pound bags of carbon. On Frank's first day, the melting foreman teamed the heat early and the third helpers needed to add over thirty bags. There were three of them so that was ten bags each. No one explained to Frank what to do or how to do it. He was expected to watch what the first two did and do the same. This meant grabbing a hundred pound bag, using the bag to shield your face by holding it high it front of you. You then walked about forty feet behind the furnace till you got close enough (about eight feet away from the spout) and then you threw the bag above the spout. Of course the paper around the carbon (charcoal) would immediately disappear. Frank's really hadn't grasped what he was supposed to do. He saw they guys ahead of him throw the bag then immediately turn back and start walking quickly away from the spout. The molten metal was so hot that flames were coming at least ten feet over the spout. Frank got as close as he thought he could, given the heat, and he threw the bag but it fell short. That was not a place where you would hear nice try, get it next time. It was more like do it again and you'll get your ass kicked. Next time Frank held it longer and made sure it went into the spout. He never missed again. When the ladle was full, a crane came in and took it away. This was not a clean process. Molten metal was still pouring out of the spout. In fact, during the open hearth process the impurities (slag) rises to the top. When the ladle is taken away there is still molten metal pouring out of the spout and now it was hitting the ground beneath the furnace. The crane came back and broke the spout away from the furnace. The second helper would put it back on for the next heat. As the slag piled up on the ground, a bulldozer and a fleet of dump trucks would pull up. This was another surreal scene. The dump truck driver would park his truck in the middle of the molten slag, and then he would get out of the cab and would start to smoke a cigarette. The bulldozer driver would drive right into the molten metal and start loading the dump truck. The dump truck had six tires that were over six feet high. All six tires would catch fire. The entire truck was completely engulfed in flames. When the bed of the truck was full, the driver would get into the truck, which by now was totally ablaze. Watching this for the first time it was a miracle that the bulldozer did not explode but is seemed like there was no way possible that the truck would not blow up. The driver would continue to smoke the cigarette, lift himself into the cab, which was now full of smoke and surrounded by flames and begin to drive away. The tires were completely engulfed in flames but after about two hundred yard the flames in the tires would begin to subside. The driver would just keep driving then exit the mill and drive to a slag dump and dump the slag. Frank used to say that there could never be a fire in the steel mill because the mill was always on fire. The entire mill was metal and dirt, neither of which could catch fire.

Frank then started to perform his other third helper function which was to control the flow of oxygen to the torch that the second helper was using. The second helper was recreating the hole after the blasting cap was thrown through the hole and the steel poured out. When the torch hit the remaining metal in the hole the second helper was consumed in a ball of sparks. Frank, fearing the worst, shut off the oxygen. The second helper looked at him and gave him a hand signal to turn it back on. Frank did, but when the second helper was once again engulfed in sparks, Frank turned it off again. This made the second helper lay down his torch and run up to Frank to tell him in no uncertain terms not to turn the oxygen off. The second helper that Frank was working with was a short, muscular black man. Frank would find out later that he was a good amateur boxer in his day. That was not surprising. Everyone in the mill seemed to be an ex-football player, boxer or Green Beret. Even when he was working the torch at the back end of the furnace, he had a cigar in his mouth. He was a man of few words and he wanted to get his job done as quickly as possible. This time Frank left the oxygen on even when the sparks were so thick that he could no longer see the second helper. Had he fallen, slipped or caught fire Frank would not have known. But that was work in the mill. It was hot, dirty, dangerous and difficult. At least it was for Frank. Frank came into the locker room about 20 minutes before the shift ended and his roommate was already there. His roommate had showered although he really didn't get dirty. Frank was so covered with soot that he could not have left the mill and gone out into the public without scaring someone. Frank's roommate was given a simple job in the mold yard; He had to look inside the molds as they passed through to see if there was any water or debris inside, before the hot steel was poured into them. If there was some water, he would blow it out with an air hose. If there was debris, he would call the crane operator to lift the mold off the rail car and remove the debris. This needed to be done about four times per shift. The rest of the time he sat in a little room with a couple other guys. Frank did not really care that his roommate has a cushy job until they got there first paychecks and his roommate made almost one hundred dollars more than him. Frank's roommate left at the end of the summer to attend law school, but Frank stayed on and finagled his way into taking his roommate's job at the mold yard.

Based on his experience in the mill, Frank could not understand the plot behind modern Gangster shows. Pittsburgh had always been a town dominated by the mob. It did not get the press like Chicago or New York, but the mob had infiltrated most aspects of society in Pittsburgh. The reason they could do this was because they had a solid foundation. That foundation was the numbers racket. That gave them the money to dominate after hours clubs, pin ball and vending machines even garbage collection. The mills provided the perfect structure to rapidly collect and payout money bet on the numbers. The payouts were always made and the numbers business ran like a well-oiled machine. The mills operated on an almost military or Napoleonic leadership structure. There was a line boss or supervisor for about every 12 people and it built up from there. The numbers racket just duplicated this structure. It seemed like every 12th man was numbers runner. Almost everyone in the mill played the numbers, some played multiple combinations for big money but most were just two dollar players. But again, that was thirty thousand potential people playing every day and that was just one mill. This provided a cash cow that financed all other mob activities. Traditional criminal activity like drugs and prostitution was really not conducted by the mob in Pittsburgh. These activities were too risky and did not provide the guaranteed profits of the numbers. The head of the mob families had long since moved beyond criminal activity (other than numbers) and no one really prosecuted that. The state finally realized they might as well join the mob and in fact this put them out of business. The mob tried to hang on by offering better payouts than the state lottery but that didn't last. That essentially ended the golden era of mob rule in Pittsburgh and Frank assumed that was what happened all over. He could not understand how the Sopranos had such a big following when the show did not make sense to him.

Frank worked in the mill with a Navy veteran and an Army Veteran. The Army veteran was the crane operator and his nickname was Smash (not good for a crane operator). He was a big, physical guy with a bad temper. He did not like to be awakened at when he was in the crane, especially if he had a hangover. Before he went up to the crane, the guys would get together in a small office at the beginning of the shift. Smash had an unlimited number of stories from his days in Vietnam. Hard to tell which were true, but he had an impressive array. He mostly told of time spent as a prison guard, watching over guys who had got caught doing all the things that he had done. The other guy in the office was a Navy Veteran. He told stories of going to the Philippines and being unable to spend $2.00 on a night on the town. Beer was a dime. A steak was fifty cents. This all seemed very exotic to Frank who had never left the country and barely traveled within the United States. Frank wanted to go to law school. He had decent grades and had a middle of the road test score. He applied to the University of Pittsburgh and through an acquaintance received an interview with the Dean. The Dean showed him a graph. Frank's test score and grades put him below the acceptance line on the graph. The dean said there was nothing he could do. He did state that if Frank was a minority, or a female or a veteran, he could probably get him in. Of the three, Frank could only affect the veteran opportunity.

In May of that year, a few things happened. Frank totaled his car after a night of drinking. For some reason he did not get a ticket or DUI but assumed his insurance would go through the roof. He received a letter from several law schools saying he was not admitted even the school where the father of a college football teammate who was an alumni wrote him a letter of recommendation but that was not enough to get him in. He was stuck in a rut. He was making good money and there was a good probability that he would get a position as a supervisor in the mill and spend the rest of his life in Pittsburgh, but that is not what he wanted. He went to the local recruiter's office, did well on the test and was accepted in to the military despite having terrible, uncorrected vision. This was the beginning of the All-Volunteer Army and things like poor eyesight were overlooked. Frank did not really research his options. He probably could have come in as an officer but did not really know the difference. The Vietnam ERA GI Bill was still being offered and military service would repay the National Defense Loans that Frank had received in college. Frank decided that he would enlist in the Army.

Chapter 13
Enlistment

Frank went to basic training and was assigned to an infantry unit in Germany. Since Frank could type he worked in the commander's office. Frank worked as the training NCO even though he was not a Noncommissioned officer (just a Spec 4). The company first sergeant was a great soldier who assembled a good team around him. The Commander's driver, the company clerk, Frank and the first sergeant really worked well together. Frank learned a lot about leadership from the first sergeant. The first sergeant had spent his entire career, to include his tours in Vietnam, with the 82d Airborne. He was all about fitness, looking sharp and aggression. He had no faith in the mechanized equipment that the unit had in Germany. He was great for a unit which had gotten soft and lazy thinking that it was their job to drive to the inter German border and clash with the Soviets in major tank battles. He instilled a warrior sprit in the unit. He was hard to pin down racially. He was not quite black, certainly not white or Hispanic. The driver even asked him one day what race he was and he just said he didn't worry about that. He was charismatic, somewhat profane and the troops loved him. In fact, Frank learned quickly that if wanted something done, he would say top wants this done and it would be done instantly. If Frank were to say the Captain wants this done, he would always get an answer like tell that Captain to go screw himself. These were tough times for the Army. It was post-Vietnam and the Army really didn't have a mission or the support of the American people. Enlistment standards were nonexistent. You could join if you didn't have high school diploma. You could join if you were a CAT 4 on the mental aptitude test. In fact there was analysis done as to whether the high school dropout was better than the CAT4s when in reality, neither should have been admitted. There was rampant drug use. Incredibly, drug abusers were not kicked out but went into a month's long rehab program that got them out of field duty. It was essentially a reward to be in the rehab program. The Army did not even test for marijuana at the time, for fear the entire force would be in rehab. The reason the All-Volunteer Army succeeded in Frank's opinion, was because African Americans joined in large numbers. It is a little known story that needs to be told. The noncommissioned officer corps after Vietnam was had a large proportion of blacks who stuck with the military and were determined to make a better life for themselves and ensure soldiers were trained and ready for the next fight.

There were not many programs in place to deal with the inevitable racial problems. This was magnified in Germany where there was often limited opportunity to go downtown for relaxation. A lot of places were off limits to GIs and probably rightly so. GIs were concentrated in mass in cities along the inter German border and could easily overwhelm a nightclub or bar. There were almost no American women in these areas. It just made for a volatile mix and not all could handle it. However good leaders could prevail and Frank's company first sergeant was the best. Despite having a unit filled with high school dropouts, most soldiers wanted to belong to an elite organization, and the first sergeant did his best to turn the unit into a replica of the units he had served with in the Airborne. He personally led the physical fitness training. He personally inspected every soldier every day. He did not worry about what the Captain or the Colonel or the General wanted. He had his standards and they were going to be applied. He was also great in the field. He ensured troops were fed and taken care of. Frank normally drove for him. They traveled throughout the German countryside in a Gamma Goat, a clumsy eight wheeled vehicle, but if properly maintained, could go anywhere a tank of Armored Personnel Carrier could go. The First Sergeant encouraged Frank to apply for Officer Candidate School. Frank just wanted to get out and go to law school. Although his grades and test scores had not changed, he was getting accepted into every school that he applied to. Being a veteran made a big difference. There was one hitch however. Frank had met a German girl and things were getting serious. Frank had joked that the only reason that she went out with him was because he kept bringing them items that he could get at the Post Exchange. Not the typical cigarettes, alcohol or other rationed items, but simple things that the Americans had perfected like Pringles potato chips, Neapolitan ice cream, soft toilet paper and big, fluffy towels. Even Crest toothpaste was big hit. Frank spoke almost perfect German and for most of his tour lived downtown.

Shortly after he arrived, the barracks he was in were being re-modeled. The troops were moved to a tent city that was terrible. Each tent had a space heater for heat that only worked if you added gasoline to the diesel and if you didn't constantly watch, it would get so hot that there was always a danger of a tent fire. Of course, bathrooms and showers were outside in trailers. They were frequently out of hot water. This was in garrison. Troops expected this in the field, but not in garrison. A four star general flew in one day and said the conditions in the tent city were unacceptable, which they were. He ordered them to be taken down. What he didn't say was where to put the troops so any soldier who had any ability to move downtown with a girlfriend or to team up with roommates was allowed to move off post. Frank jumped at the chance and this really allowed him to immerse himself in all things German. He bought a small car (an Audi NSU) that had an 800cc engine. On a date with his future wife, he shifted from first to second, gunned the engine and his future wife ended up in the back seat. The car was starting to rust and the rails that held the front seat to the body of the car broke loose when Frank shifted. At first he didn't notice, but his future wife was lying flat in the back seat looking up at the ceiling. Frank got some bondo and fixed it but his girlfriend never really trusted it again. It was a typical GI car. Purchased for $300 with a $250 stereo in it. It could only go 55 MPH. Frank was talking with his girlfriend's brother and he told him that it had taken him 3 hours to go from Schweinfurt to the Frankfurt Airport. His girlfriend's brother was incredulous. It should only take less than an hour and one half. . Frank said there was no traffic. They even got out a map to ensure Frank did not take the wrong route and he didn't. Then Frank went for a ride with his future brother in law. He was a typical German and once on the autobahn he was a zwei hundert fahrer, meaning he drove 200 kilometers per hour or 120 miles per hour. That explained the difference in drive time to Frankfurt.

Frank also found that he enjoyed being in the Army. He liked the physical fitness component and given his English degree he was always in demand to write awards and efficiency reports and he was really good at it. Frank did apply for OCS and was accepted. He arrived at Fort Benning after being told horror stories by all of the Officers who had attended OCS during the Vietnam War, where they would accept almost everyone then washout about 50 percent. From the first day that Frank arrived, he had no doubt that he would excel. Most of the candidates were from logistical, medical or intel units. A lot were just plain out of shape. OCS was at the home of the infantry and Frank has just left an infantry unit. He was in shape, knew weapons inside and out and was good at map reading. In fact, right before he attended OCS, he was selected to attend

French Commando School. Frank was selected because of his ability to speak German. The Lieutenant in charge could speak French and since the school was actually located in Germany (although run by the French) a lot of the French trainers spoke German and Frank would interpret. The last week of the course involved an insertion into the Black Forest and the American Platoon that was going through the course was essentially required to live off the land while avoiding detection by the aggressors. That meant marching all night. The French speaking American lieutenant would receive orders over the radio and the platoon would walk all night carrying everything on their backs. It was brutally cold (February) with snow on the ground, which made marching at night with packs difficult. The platoon would stop to rest but would instantly start to freeze. The only option was to keep marching. The platoon members would grab the rucksack of the man in front of them and literally fall asleep while walking. The platoon was supposed to lay low during the day but ended up marching most of the day. They suspected it was because our lieutenant was lost. The third night confirmed their suspicions. They walked almost twenty kilometers that night and when the sun came up they could see that they had only gone about 400 meters from where they started. At that point our NCO took the map (he was a Green Beret in Vietnam) and he led us the rest of the way. The commando school was a great preparation for OCS.

When Frank arrived at OCS, he expected to find 250 people absolutely consumed with becoming a second lieutenant and willing to endure any ordeal to get there. That was not the case. Most were normal people, all with certain talents and abilities. All wanted to succeed, but that would not get in the way of having a good time under the circumstances. Frank was fortunate to get a good TAC officer. He had two roommates and they all became really close friends. One had always excelled academically and both he and his brother were in the OCS class. They had both graduated from college several years ahead of their peers. The older brother was nineteen and looked and acted fairly mature. The younger brother was in Frank's platoon. He graduated from college at 18 and he looked younger. He was incredibly smart and physically fit. Both of the boys had grown up on a ranch in Arizona and they were very conservative. Frank had really never known a conservative young person, growing up in Pittsburgh with the heavy union presence, virtually all local politicians were Democrats. Frank's roommate used to say that Richard Nixon was a saint. He idolized Nixon. This was after he was impeached. Frank had never heard another person say anything good about Nixon. There was no question that they would graduate. It would remain to be seen how a platoon of infantry would respond to an 18 year old in charge.

Frank also arrived having spent the last two years in Germany. During that time he did not read any newspapers or watch even one TV show. He had been in a cultural vacuum. One the first day, one of the guys in the platoon was imitating John Belushi's Samurai chef routine. Frank thought he was a professional comedian. He had never seen or even heard of Saturday Night Live. Later in the program all of the platoons had to do a skit, and one of the platoons did a version of Sixty Minutes, another program Frank had never seen. Of course, while in OCS there was no access to television, newspapers or even radio. The class did have women in it. Frank had come from the infantry where there were no women. The Women's Army Corps has just disbanded and women were in the class. Frank was in first platoon and there were 10 women out of the 30 candidate's in the platoon. There was also a female TAC officer. She was the TAC for 2d Platoon but that didn't stop her from getting on Frank if she noticed him fidgeting in formation.

Frank was one of the most physically fit persons in the class and he assumed that alone would carry him through. He began piling up demerits for not folding his clothes properly and not making his bed so that a quarter could be bounced off of it. When his TAC said he needed to tighten things up, Frank stated that when they did the five mile run or the twenty mile ruck march with full pack, half the class wouldn't make it and he would rise to the top. The TAC said there will be no five mile run and there will be no 20 mile ruck march. Everything is being done in three ability groups and the third group's standards are so low that it is doubtful that anyone would be kicked out for fitness, men or women. Frank started folding his clothes and making his bed to standard at that point.

Frank was on a running team that allowed him to travel for road races and get out of Fort Benning. They wore white T shirts with their last name stenciled in the center. They had shorts with an OCS insignia, but the O was on the outside of the CS and there was no way you could surmise that the emblem was OCS unless someone told you. The team traveled to Plains, Georgia (home of Jimmy Carter) for a 10K race. Everyone who asked Frank where he and his teammates were from got the same answer: the prison. With their short cropped hair and good builds no one questioned this. Everyone gave Frank and his teammates a lot of room that day.

OCS also exposed Frank to one of the more bizarre aspects of Army leadership. That was the top 5 and bottom 5. Every week all members of the platoon had to place 5 teammates in the top and 5 in the bottom. It was as if some must fail and some must excel when conditions should be set to allow all to succeed. He started putting people in the top 5 for bizarre reasons assuming that most people would place this same folks in the bottom. Frank placed one guy in the top 5 because he snuck out at night and brought Arby's Roast Beef sandwiches for the platoon. That guy showed real leadership and caring for the troops. Frank could not tell the TAC the reason he placed him first or he would have got in trouble, but Frank used other examples to prove that this guy was number 1. It still amazed Frank in the Army must have a few succeed and a few fail. It does not have to be this way. Even when Frank was in an airborne unit, where everyone was a superstar, someone had to fail and not get promoted.

Frank was used to group punishment and was no stranger to corporal punishment and was quite surprised that the Army did not hit soldiers either in basic training or in OCS. Frank attended a Catholic grade school and would say that 8 years at that elementary school cured him of religion. Since he was the oldest of six kids, there was no question about where he would attend grade school. His family was Irish Catholic. His grandparents had come over on the boat from Ireland and his Uncle (his dad's brother) was a priest. Frank actually enjoyed attending the school. There were only two classes in each grade and he made friends easily. He did endure the typical corporal punishment that came with a Catholic school. One of the things Frank and all others had to put up with was the group punishment. The nuns were expert at that and at psychological warfare. When Frank was in the early grades, the nuns would really put the pressure on to donate money to their causes. Every year they had a drive to save the pagan babies. Of course they had a terrible tale to tell about these pagan babies. They never really said where they were from, but the pagan babies could not attend Mass and that had to be corrected with money raised from the students. Most students were working class and since they were Catholic, they typically had four or five brothers and or sisters, who were also attending the school, and subject to the same pressures to support the pagan babies. The school specialized in Irish twins and a lot of the families would have runs of kids in three or four grades in a row. To up the pressure, the nuns had paper cutouts of the pagan babies. They would write the names of all the students on the blackboard and then place a pagan baby by the name each time a donation of a dollar was made. One or two students would donate 10 or 15 dollars and have that many pagan babies placed in a row by their name. This made it real easy for the nuns to pressure the students that only had one or zero. They would make first and second graders feel like they were personally responsible for pagan babies starving and not being converted. Bringing children to tears seemed to be the goal of this drill. It was very effective however. If kids couldn't wring money out of their parents, they would collect empty soda bottles to raise money so that they would have at least a few pagan babies by their name. Frank didn't mind the corporal punishment. His dad was a huge bear of a man who dished out punishment whether you needed it or not. Even when he was playing, his roughhousing hurt. There was nothing the nuns could do that could compete. He was however surprised by the randomness of the attacks. He had a nun in third grade that had long passed her time for being an effective teacher. She taught math, but her idea of teaching math was to have students practice making brackets. The class spent a year doing this. To please her, they had to be perfect and the students would really concentrate on making them just right. She would sneak up behind an unsuspecting boy and if she didn't approve of the brackets, she would jab her index finger into the back of a boy's head. It felt like a drill bit going into the brain. Even Frank had to admit that hurt.

One of the things drilled into all students was that you had to give the nuns a lot of space. If you touched a nun's habit that was a cardinal sin (as opposed to a venial sin) on you, regardless of the circumstances. If a nun backed into you or if your elbow was sticking out and you brushed against the nun's habit that was a sin on you. This was reinforced daily in the early years of school. This stuck with Frank and when he attended a Catholic College that training kicked back in. The college had German nuns who prepared and served the food. On one of Frank's first days in the cafeteria at lunch, one of the nuns was refilling the milk machine and one of the students snuck up behind her lifted her rope and looped it around the handle of the adjoining milk machine. When the nun went to move away, the rope tightened and pulled her back towards the machine. Everyone had a nice little laugh. Everyone except Frank. Frank's training from grade school kicked in. Someone had actually touched a nun's habit on purpose. Frank could not imagine the consequences of that act. But even the nun herself smiled, unwrapped her rope and went about her business. Frank remained in shock.

The group punishment at grade school remained throughout the full eight years. When Frank was in eighth grade, his class went outside for recess and started throwing snowballs. This was not allowed, so all the boys were lined up in the cafeteria. There was no attempt to determine who had actually thrown the snowballs. They were all going to get punished. This breach of discipline required that the principal get involved. The boys were 13 years and some were approaching six feet tall. The principal strode into the room. She was fresh off serving in a mission to Brazil. She must have been deep in the jungle with limited access to food, because she was about four feet nine inches tall and weighed about 80 pounds. There were 40 boys lined up single file. The nun did not give a speech or talk to anyone. She just walked up to the first boy and in one sweeping motion slapped him across the face four times, then moved to the next boy. The first 10 boys really got slapped hard. But it is not easy to smack forty boys across the face, especially if your hand was nothing but bone. Of course, once committed, there was not stopping. The last twenty or so only received gentle taps. Her hand was throbbing and may in fact have been broken. No one smiled or laughed though because the next step after the principal would have been the priest and he certainly would not have had a problem smacking a few eighth graders. The group punishment continued. In one grading period every boy received a D in Math and an unsat in conduct and an unsat in effort. Frank's father was furious and Frank knew better than to blame the grades on the teacher. He did get his mom to go to the school and tell the principal that Frank wanted to attend South Catholic, but would not get in if grades were handed out on emotion rather than performance. After that, he had no problem. Frank had no intention of going to South Catholic. They had brothers rather than nuns and that really ratcheted up the corporal punishment. There was no way Frank was going to attend South Catholic. Two things worked in his favor. One was the high tuition and money was always tight with six kids. The other thing was that Frank told his dad that he was a year behind the public school kids in math and would have to go to summer school and take Algebra to catch up. The public school was large and progressive and good students could take advanced courses. Even Frank's dad couldn't square that. He kept the next three sisters in catholic school but when Frank's youngest sister came home from first grade in tears, even he had had enough. He pulled all the kids out and sent them to the public school. The priest even came to the house to try to get him to change his mind, but even Frank's dad changed his views about corporal punishment and psychological mistreatment faster than the school had.

As he was nearing graduation from OCS, Frank had to pick a branch. Frank drew on his enlisted experience. One thing serving in the Infantry had taught him was that there was too much standing around waiting and too much objectivity. He noticed that the mechanics, truck drivers and supply people liked their jobs and were good at them. They still went to the rifle range and did the Army things, but no one really bothered them during the day. They just went to work. Everyone assumed that Frank would go airborne, ranger, infantry and he feigned disappointment at getting quartermaster but that was what he wanted. Even with that he was able to walk across the street and enroll on airborne school right after graduation.

Chapter 14

Monterey

Prior to his commissioning, most of Frank's leadership training had come from playing football at College, working at United States Steel and watching his first sergeant get things accomplished while assigned to an infantry unit in Germany. What they have in common was a hands on approach to leadership. It involved knowing your job, doing it well, ensuring that other could count on your words and deeds. Officer Candidate School was somewhat disappointing in the formal leadership training, but the informal leadership displayed by the students was very informative.

Frank's first assignment as a lieutenant was to a maintenance company in Fort Ord California. The company was a huge organization with seven platoons, which meant there were seven lieutenants and six warrant officers. The unit was attached to the 707th maintenance battalion but supported all the non-divisional units (units that were on Fort Ord but not assigned to the 7th Infantry Division. Frank spent almost four years in the company. This was very rare, but it provided a solid foundation for Frank to learn his craft. It also exposed him to three separate company commanders, who certainly had contrasting styles. The company was always an exceptional unit and that was due to the warrant officers. Most had been in that unit for several years and they were expert in their areas. They were quite an eclectic mix. There was a former German officer, who joined the American Army and became a warrant officer. He was meticulous and incredibly organized. There was a warrant of Japanese ancestry who ran the shop. We also had a fiery Puerto Rican who maintained the engineer equipment and a Hawaiian who did the welding and body work. They were great with lieutenants, letting them lead but not letting them do anything that didn't make sense. They always ensured the company excelled. Frank was the only lieutenant that did not have a warrant officer signed to his section, and he did spend some time learning what was expected of his unit. His job was to run the tech supply, the organization that provided repairs parts for all the shops in the company. He had good troops and a good non-commissioned officer. He was also on the cutting edge of computer-ization and he took to that very well.

The unit was selected to conduct an exercise at the Yakima Training Center in Washington state. It was quite an event and an-other career building operation. The unit had to convoy from Fort Ord to Yakima, Washington. The convoy consisted of almost three hundred vehicles. Originally it was planned to take three days but ended up taking four days. As the convoy was lining up, the battalion commander did a walk through and noticed that our contact trucks (a variation of a Chevy Blazer) had CB radios installed. All of the drivers were mechanics and the truck had a vast array of tools and test equipment in the back. These mechanics had gotten together and thought it would be a good idea to have CB radios because here were no military radios available and they assumed correctly that that they would be strung out repairing vehicles from Fort Ord to Yakima. The battalion commander ordered them to remove the ra-dios. As soon as the convoy moved out though, it was apparent that the unit did not have the communications to control such a large movement. About two hours into the trip the convoy was trying to negotiate through Sacramento and about twenty of the trucks took a wrong turn and headed for Reno. The trucks had no communication and the command vehicles were M151 jeeps. There was no way that a jeep pulling a trailer could catch a line haul truck rolling down the highway. The battalion commander rescinded his order and allowed the use of the CB radios. Eventually all the trucks got headed in the right direction. One of the other maintenance company commanders was driving along the highway when the left wheel of his trailer fell off. This was a maintenance company commander but he couldn't even keep his own vehicle intact. The Captain didn't notice what had happened and he drove for almost ten miles shooting sparks from where the axel on the trailer was striking the road surface. These sparks flew into the median and caught the median on fire. This was California in August and any little spark was enough to start a grass fire. Truckers going the other way were on the radios warning oncoming traffic. The smoke got so bad that the interstate had to be shut down. The Captain was oblivious.

Travelling to Yakima was almost a religious experience. The convoy went right by Mount Shasta and Frank has never seen anything so breathtaking. They stayed overnight in a National Park near Klamath Falls Oregon, also beautiful. When they got to Washington state, the convoy turned west and traveled along the Colombia River Gorge. The convoy drove right by Mount St Helens and the remnants of the volcano damage could still be seen. That trip, plus the opportunity to live in Monterey, California, was a unique experience that made serving in the military such a great profession. An assignment to Fort Ord allowed normal people to live in one of the most beautiful and expensive places on earth. Not only could you live there, but live well. Most lived on base and shopped at the commissary so the high cost of living was not a factor. All of the lieutenants Frank knew had sports cars and motorcycles, took ski trips to Lake Tahoe, went surfing in Santa Cruz and scuba diving in Monterey Bay. It was truly life style of the rich and famous on a military pay check. Frank's wife worked in Carmel Valley at a resort where wealthy women came to lose weight. It was an absolute paradise. Her boss was a little strange, a typical Californian who said she had to take a lot of medicinal herbs to get her through the day. It was a family oriented business and Frank's wife did a little of everything to include preparing the meals. Frank was allowed to visit on the weekends and use the pool. He even ended up doing the taxes for the business. His wife had always been a horseback rider and was quite accomplished in dressage. She was able to ride at a horse ranch in Carmel Valley on her way to and from work. That assignment to Fort Ord was truly unique, but was probably duplicated in places like Coronado, Tampa, Hawaii, and other places that were considered vacation spots but where the military actually had a major presence. Also Fort Ord was actually a resort area. The weather was always great. Not too hot, not too cold. In fact, when Frank was first assigned to Fort Ord, he rented an apartment in Salinas. He never needed heat or air conditioning. His electric bill often was less than $10 per month. Soldiers would volunteer for field duty, unlike in Germany where winter maneuvers were brutal and most soldiers tried every excuse to get out of field duty. At Fort Ord, most of the exercises were done at a national park that was next to Camp Roberts, by the Soledad prison. It was like Frank had walked into a new organization.

The lack of Captains at Fort Ord was a bonus for the lieutenants. There were seven companies in the battalion and at one point six were commanded by senior lieutenants. There was an unwritten rule that you should be a Captain and a graduate of the advanced course to command a company. The new Battalion Commander selected Frank's friend to be the new Commander of the unit. Even though it was the largest unit in the Battalion, the new commander could see that the lieutenant he selected, who was serving as his adjutant, was up to the job. In fact he was almost a carbon copy of the new battalion commander. He also was incredibly physically fit and he set high standards for himself and would quite certainly set high standards for a unit under his command. His first action in taking over the company was setting up the change of command inventory. The battalion commander assigned a warrant officer to manage the property book and he confirmed how bad the situation was. The unit had 250 general mechanics tool box. Everything in that tool box could be used for a commercial purpose. The unit also had a machine shop and shops sets that included very expensive technical tools to include torque wrenches. These items were just plain missing. In a unit that size, it did not take long to get into the tens of thousands of dollars. The new commander conducted a thorough inventory and made sure he had everything that was short on order. He was always following up with monthly inventories. Also Frank had changed jobs and was now the shop officer, responsible for the mission. Frank knew that the inventories were a necessary evil but at least the commander gave him plenty of warning so he could adjust work schedules. He was meticulous in everything he did.

The unit was designated as a rapid deployment force unit. The new commander scheduled a field exercise, but instead of sending the unit out to dig foxholes, he sent a small team to the field to a place where there were mock ups of the Air Force strategic aircraft. Frank was the mobility officer and the commander told him to set it up. Each platoon rolled through the mockups to validate their load plans. The unit was certainly ready to deploy. Less than two weeks later, the unit was alerted. A C5 (the largest plane in the Air Force Inventory) landed and the unit was tasked to send three platoons out to the airfield and load their equipment. To this day, Frank says he thinks his commander was psychic. It is was the most timely example of executing a relevant training exercise that was almost immediately implemented.

The next commander could not have been more different. He

was an older Captain who had spent a lot of time as an enlisted man. He truly enjoyed commanding soldiers and he was good at it. Since the unit was one of the largest on the base, he stated that meant we should win everything starting with sports competitions. Almost daily he would call Frank at the shop and remind him that he was late for football practice. If there was a trophy up for grabs, the Captain was going to win it and he usually did. The company had the best football team, the best motor pool and the best reenlistment rate. Morale was sky high. He was always giving troops time off and he was genuinely funny and the troops liked him and worked hard for him. One of the things he did when he first got to Fort Ord about a year prior to taking command, was that he purchased a commercial fishing boat and leased it to some sailors. He thought this would make him a fortune. On the first trip, the sailors he hired got drunk and grounded the boat. They tore up the engine and the boat sat in the water, lifeless, for over a year. On the day he took command, he contracted a huge truck to move his boat into the vast shop complex where the company did operations. The boat could be seen from the road. It had an almost thirty foot mast. At that time you could not work on your car or motorcycle in the shop area. You could not even borrow the hand tools. These rules were strictly enforced. But that Captain had other plans. He linked up with a mechanic who taught automotive technology on base for Salinas Community College. The troops could take classes and obtain certifications and college credits. The captain had the instructor, a German, with a severe U boat commander accent, take a look at the boat and design classes around everything that needed repair. The instructor designed classes on fiberglass repair, engine rebuild, fuel pump repair, electronics repair, using the boat as the teaching aide. In six months, the boat was like new and most of the troops in the unit received three credit hours in automotive technology for working on his boat. At one point, the division commander came though the shops on an unannounced visit. The Captain came down to walk him through the shop. Frank was convinced the Captain would get chewed out because of the boat, but the Captain liked operating at high levels. He played golf with the Colonels and Generals on base. They were about the same age, and he even wrangled a house on base that was close to the Generals. When the General came through, the Captain explained what he was doing, tied the classes to the reenlistment rate, which was the highest on post and by the end of the tour, the Captain and the General were smoking cigars and the Captain has promised to take the General on the maiden voyage, which he did.

Frank was selected to command a forward support maintenance company tasked to support the 1st Brigade of the 7th Infantry Division. The Brigade was commanded by a Colonel who was not happy with the support he was getting and didn't mind telling the DISCOM commander about it at every opportunity. The battalion commander selected Frank to command the unit. He thought Frank with his four years' experience running the largest maintenance shop on post could support this brigade commander. Shortly into his command, Frank had an office call with the Colonel. The Brigade Commander gave him some sound advice. He told Frank that he was a commander just like he was. That gave him an open door to come into the Colonel's office and question anything that he did not think correct. The Colonel told Frank that if he failed a mission or did not provide adequate support because of something the Colonel's staff said or did, the Colonel would smoke him. He understood the role of staffs and the role of commanders and he expected Frank to understand the role as well. Frank actually took him up on it when the brigade was getting ready to conduct a major exercise in Korea. The brigade headquarters and two battalions were deploying to Korea. Frank's unit was not designed to support split operations. The staff wanted Frank to leave a robust stay behind party at Fort

Ord to support the unit that was not deploying with the brigade. Frank told the Colonel that he did not agree with this, that he would send the best possible support package to Korea to ensure success of that exercise and essentially leave the one unit on Fort Ord to be supported by the installation staff. The colonel said he agreed, the exercise in Korea was the priority. The exercise was a huge success. Frank had a good relationship with the Colonel. He attended all the brigades functions and was more a part of the brigade that the DISCOM. Eventually the Army would organize so that the support units worked directly for the Combat Brigade commander, and that was essentially what Frank was doing anyway.

Frank had purchased a brand new Honda Hawk 400 motorcycle as soon as he arrived at Fort Ord. Fort Ord was a great place for motorcycles. Frank drove his motorcycle every day from Salinas to Fort Ord (13 miles) and from April to December never once got caught in the rain, mostly because it doesn't rain in California during the spring, summer and fall. That did not mean he never got wet however. One thing about Monterey is that incredibly thick fog rolls in during the summer. Frank would often pass through a fog bank on the way to work and arrive soaking wet. It could be clear and sunny at Fort Ord, but if you hit as fog bank heading to work you would get soaked. It was a small price to pay however for being able to drive a motorcycle year round. On Saturdays Frank receive his Sports Illustrated magazine in the mail (his wife typically worked on Saturday's) and he would go to the shoppette, buy something to eat and drink and head out on his motorcycle to his favorite place in the canyons of Carmel Valley. There was a spot that he particularly enjoyed that was on the crest of a mountain. The road ended at the crest and from the top you could literally see for more than 15 miles back down the road you just came up. It was a beautiful spot and very relaxing. While Frank was there a British couple drove up and started a conversation with Frank. They were bird watchers and were chasing a rare bird. Frank thought that that was a great way to get away from the normal stress of the military and he started to engage in birdwatching.

One great thing about the military is that you always had time off. The military is forever creating a three day weekend, turning a three day weekend into a four day weekend, giving soldiers time off for pay day activities or family time to compensate for the weekends and long hours endured during training exercises. All this resulted in days off when the rest of the world was at work. On one of these days off, Frank and a fellow lieutenant decided to take their motorcycles down Highway One to Big Sur. It was about a two hour drive through some of the world' most breathtaking scenery. They brought along baseball gloves and a softball to throw around when they got on the beach. When they arrived at Big Sur, the beach was deserted with the exception of two girls who were sunbathing. They got off their bikes and started throwing the softball around doing their best not to gawk at the sunbathing girls. To their surprise, the girls came up to them and asked if they could play. They used a kelp stalk as a bat and they played a form of rounders with the two girls for about an hour. If they could have filmed that for the Army, the Army would never had had any problem recruiting soldiers. On your day off, drive your motorcycle to one of the most beautiful places on earth and play a game of softball with two gorgeous girls. Just another day in paradise on a military salary.

Chapter 15
Europe

Frank's follow on assignment was to the Army Materiel Command in Europe. Compared to his first assignment as an enlisted man in the Infantry this was like paradise. He was stationed in Mannheim and worked in an organization that was mostly civilian and most of them were female. In Schweinfurt, other than a very few soldiers in the Personnel Detachment there were almost no females and he did not recall seeing any civilian employees. In fact, he ran in a track meet in Nurnberg at what was referred to as the Hitler Stadion. While he was there, a women's softball tournament going on. Frank was absolutely amazed there were enough women in Europe to field a team let alone have a tournament. The Army Materiel Command worked a 40 hour work week, did not go to the field and when they did travel they were TDY and stayed in hotels, This was a whole new world for Frank and had he known there were units in Europe like this when he was enlisted he probably would have revolted. By this time Frank was married and had one child and his wife enjoyed returning to Europe. Schweinfurt was an easy dive up A81, a beautiful relatively lightly used stretch of Autobahn that is a must drive for any car aficionado. Like most autobahns, it has no speed limit, but unlike most autobahns it did not have much traffic and you could really open it up. Frank had a Camaro and while it wasn't very fast compared to the German cars, it did handle well and was a joy to drive over there. Frank took to the staff work well and served in plans and exercises. On this tour he was really able to enjoy Europe. His wife and daughter spent a week in Schweinfurt and Frank decided to attend a learn to ski week in Chiemisee, a beautiful Armed Forces Recreation Center on Lake Chiemsee in the German Alps. Since Frank could ski he signed up with a fairly advanced group. On the first day they met in the parking lot and their guide, a New Zealander, gave them a short rules brief. He said there would be no smoking on the trip as he lit a cigarette, he said there would be no drinking on the trip as he cracked open a beer and he said we could either ski with him or ski by ourselves, but that the bus would depart the ski resort at 1630 and if you weren't there he would assume that you met up with a bird (his word for female) and that the bus would leave promptly. The first day they went to a resort in Austria. There were two Navy seals in the group. They were not experienced skiers but they were very athletic and absolutely fearless and by the end of the day they had no problem keeping up with the rest of the group. At 1630 we loaded the bus and started to leave even though there were two soldiers missing. Frank did say to the guide that maybe we should wait a while given that we were in another country. He vetoed that and the bus took off. The next morning Frank saw the two missing soldiers at breakfast. He asked them where they were yesterday. They stated that they did meet some girls and were having a few drinks and lost track of time. Frank asked how they got home and they said they hitchhiked. Frank said with your skis and the said that was no problem as almost every car had a ski rack. Frank then asked them how they knew the way back from Austria to Chiemsee. They said they didn't and in fact since they did not speak German, they were able to hitch a ride with two young guys were going right past Chiemsee. Only an American GI could pull that off.

Frank was selected to be the Commanding General's Aide toward the end of the tour. He was selected because he could speak German and the General had never served in Germany. The first order of business was to buy the general a car big enough to haul around his wife and kids. Mannheim has a business near the base that repossessed American cars from GIs and there was a minivan there that suited the General perfectly. Frank purchased the minivan and while his kids joked that it was the tan van and that it was passed by every car and most trucks on the autobahn, it was one of the few vehicles in Germany that could haul his family in one trip.

The command had widely dispersed units, so the General, the driver and Frank travelled all over Europe and since the General did not like to fly, they made good use of the Ford LTD with the trooper engine on the autobahns. The driver was a real pro and Frank and the driver made a good team.

Frank always volunteered for duty in Germany and as he attended Command and General Staff College in Leavenworth, Kansas, he told the assignments officer he wanted an assignment to Germany and was one of the first to get his orders. Frank had wanted to go to a divisional assignment in Germany but was told that he had to serve a penance as a personnel officer for at least one year. At about this time Frank was selected to be the logistician on a ten man team that was selected to go to Hamburg, Germany to participate in a war game with the equivalent German Staff Officer School in Hamburg. Frank made friends with the engineer on the team and they had a great time exploring the Reeperbahn and taking advantage of the free beer at the German officer's club. The actual war game was strange in that the Germans were very impressed with the ability of the team to quickly prepare military plans and orders. The team stated that we just modeled ourselves after what the German Army did in World War II. As part of their trip, the team took of a tour to Scherinn, in what was East Germany, but since the wall had come down was now merged with Germany. The team was told not to have any contact with the Russian troops that were still stationed there. Even though the wall had come down, Russian troops were still in garrisons in the former East Germany because there was no place for them to return to in Russia. Of course when the team was touring they immediately linked up with the Russian troops and started exchanging gear. Russian troops was a misnomer. Unknown to most U.S soldiers at the time was that the Soviet Union consisted of all of the various Stans and for some reason the troops from the Stans were the predominate soldiers in that area of East Germany. There were several unique things about this. All the Soviet soldiers from the Stans were draftees and they were all about 5 feet tall. They looked more Asian than Caucasian. They did not speak Russian, German or English. It was like they had been transported another world. It was hard to imagine how this amalgamation of third world peoples who did not speak a common language could have been considered an effective fighting force. Regardless, we all traded our uniform items for Russian coats, hats, belt buckles and insignia. Also while we were in the former East Germany, the team went into a restaurant. Being typical Americans, the team members were asking the waitress if they could mix and match items on the menu. She was young and good looking and they guys starting flirting with her. She still was in the old communist ways and was reluctant to deviate from the norm. Frank served as the interpreter and basically convinced her to give the guys what they wanted even though it would virtually destroy the inventory process used by the restaurant. The waitress drew the line when it came to dessert, however. One of the guys wanted pie and ice cream. The waitress said this would be impossible. She got into discussion with Frank as to how the hot pie would melt the cold ice cream and that these westerners must be the dumbest people on the face of the earth if they couldn't figure that out. She also told Frank that if the Americans and others from the west were going to come over and rewrite all the rules and disturb the norm she was not sure if it was worth it. For Frank who had spent six years in Germany travelling to fighting positions on the inter German border it was an amazing experience to drive into the former East Germany and actually mingle with the former enemy.

Frank's year spent working in personnel was most difficult assignment in his career. He certainly was not a people person, but that was not what made the job difficult. Since the wall had come down, the Army was in the process of eliminating over half of the units in Germany and sending them back to the states. The Army was sending almost 100,000 soldiers from Germany to America while simultaneously sending soldiers to Germany. This created a personnel mess where some units were vastly over strength while others were critically short and caused Frank to constantly be moving personnel from one location to another within Germany Even with the glut of soldiers returning, Frank's logistic accounts had shortages everywhere and field commanders were constantly calling and complaining that they did not have enough Captains, Majors and Lieutenant Colonels. Also, from the time that Frank arrived at his desk at around 0700 in the morning the phone would be ringing and the person on the line would be a soldier with a problem. The entire day was spent listening to a valid complaint on the phone; usually from a soldier in the states who didn't have orders, and trying to process paperwork while talking on the phone. It was incredibly stressful. The only good thing about the assignment was that the officers who worked in officer assignments were not personnel officers even though they were in a personnel command. The assignment officers working with Frank were the only officers not in the Adjutant General Corps and they all knew they would be going back to their basic branch at soon as that tour was over. There were a lot of nuances that made that assignment unique, but Frank and the guys in the office did not have to get involved in Adjutant General Corps politics. They just had to survive their year as an assignment officer. There was as infantry officer, an aviator, an engineer, a field artillery officer and Frank as the logistician. Some of the others had to double up to cover the MPs, Special Forces and smaller branches. The Infantry officer ran his desk like he was operating out of the back of an armored personnel carrier during a field exercise. From the time he arrived to the time he left he would be on the phone screaming at whoever was calling. He almost never sat down. He would yell at the clerks and he would use a headphone so that he could move around when he was on the phone but invariably he would forget he was connected the phone and when he would walk away from his desk the phone would fly across the desk, taking all his paperwork and spewing it onto the floor. This would send him into an even higher hover. The clerks were terrified of him. If any of the assignment officers had to stay for more than one year, they would have been committed to an insane asylum. One good thing about the job was that the boss was an infantry colonel who had earned the Silver Star in Vietnam and was good friends with the US Army Europe Commander, who was a four star general. That gave the team the ultimate top cover. As long as they cleared what we were doing with him, he would back the team when the field commanders would call complaining that they were being shorted with officers. Frank became fast friends with the Colonel. They were both members of the Heidelberg Ski Club. Frank would team up with him and sponsor one of the ski trips as the trip captains. The Colonel had a bad knee and did not ski but he would go on the trip. The trip captains did not have to pay for the trip, but had to organize it, so Frank always picked the most expensive trip to Switzerland. The Colonel would do all the recruiting and Frank would collect the money and make all the arrangements. The Colonel was in tight with all of the expats in the Heidelberg area and would get all kinds of donations to be given away during the bus ride to the ski resort. It was always a guarantee that the trip would sell out instantly because the ski club members knew that the Colonel would be giving away bottles of Jack Daniels, T shirts, Ski gear, all donated by his buddies. The Colonel also attended the running of the bulls every year, but Frank never attended that with him. If Frank would have done that in all likelihood his wife would have said that he crossed the line. She didn't mind the one ski trip and she let him go to the Saturday rugby matches, but that was about all she would tolerate. She expected Frank to coach the kid's athletic events and help them with their schoolwork, which he did.

Frank had gone to CGSC at Fort Leavenworth with one of the other assignment officers and they became good friends. The command chaplain was sponsoring a trip to Switzerland that was called a Duty Day with God. They both received permission to go. The intent was once in Geneva they would slip away and go to a bar. When Frank asked his friend if he had ever been to Geneva and if he knew where they could go, the he said that all European cities were the same. There was a church, a castle, a river and a red light district with bars and he had no doubt he could find the red light district. We loaded up on three buses and departed. The bus Frank was on got separated from the other two busses and when the bus driver got to the outskirts of Geneva he pulled over and asked the sergeant who was the chaplain's assistant (and tentatively in charge) where we were supposed to go. The first stop was supposed to be a Swiss military barracks, but the sergeant had no idea where that was. At that point, he asked who was the highest-ranking person of the bus. Everyone looked at one another and quickly determined it was Frank. He had now gone from innocent bystander to being in charge of a bus that was lost in Switzerland. Again, Frank used his ability to speak German, got out a map and he and the bus driver plotted a route to get to the barracks. They arrived before the other two busses. The chaplain on the other bus was so worried that he had called the US Embassy in Switzerland to report that he had lost a bus load of American soldiers. For the rest of Frank's tour the chaplain would tell him how grateful he was that Frank had taken charge and got the bus where it needed to go.

The Swiss Army is quite unique. Everyone serves and they are very professional even though they maintain strict neutrality. The soldiers were incredibly physically fit and when we were done with our tour of the compound, the soldiers said they would demonstrate the downhill run. The barracks was at the top of an 8,000 foot mountain, and they said a platoon of soldiers would race the bus to the bottom. Of course the bus had numerous switchbacks but it was amazing to watch the soldiers run in what could be described as a controlled fall down the side of the mountain. Of course they beat the bus by several minutes. It was an incredible display.

One of the very few highlights of the tour at the Personnel Command was that Frank and one of the other officers went back to Leavenworth to talk to the Majors that were coming to Europe. Prior to leaving, the Engineer Assignments Officer told Frank to take care of his buddy, an Ordnance Officer in Frank's account. Frank had never met him. Frank interviewed all of the officers heading for Germany. Since he had large accounts and he had vacancies everywhere, he was able to give everyone what they wanted. Some wanted to work in Heidelberg on the staff initially and some even wanted to take less glamorous jobs in the Netherlands. Not everyone wanted to go to the divisions or armored cavalry regiments. Frank was almost finished and the ordnance officer had yet to show up. Finally, the last interview on the last day he showed up with his wife. They had just recently married and his wife had heard all the stories that home is where the Army sends you. When they walked in Frank immediately asked where do you want to go. He said I can give you any assignment you want. Heidelberg, 3ID, 1st AD, 3rd

ACR, Bavaria, Frankfurt, Netherlands. Wherever. He was taken aback by the choices. His wife could not believe it. Frank then mentioned that his good buddy said to take care of him so that is what he was doing. He asked for an assignment in the 3ID so that he could return with his new bride to Bavaria. Frank locked it in right then and there. He didn't really see him until three years later when the both showed up at the guest house at Fort Bragg on the same day. He and Frank were both selected to command airborne battalions in the COSCOM. Since he had been in the airborne before, he showed Frank all of the nuances of wearing the beret which included taking it in the shower, shaping it on your head while it was wet, drying it out while shaped, cutting the inside of the lining out and using a razor to shave the beret. Frank complied because he didn't want to look like Chef Boy Ar Dee on his first day. The wives became great friends and they even ended up being assigned together to the Pentagon after their command tours.

Chapter 16
Government Service

Frank transitioned from being a contractor on the Joint Staff to a government civilian about one year after he returned from Iraq in 2006. He liked to say he held out for less money and fewer benefits. The contractor world could provide a good package that augmented military retirement. Government service did not. Frank had health care from the military thanks to his retirement by did not have dental and he did receive less pay. He did get a little more job security however. Even with two wars going on contracts still had to be competed and there was always a chance your company could lose the contract. Frank continued to go to Walter Reed. In fact he had gone so often that he was one of the few that mastered how to get from the Pentagon to Walter Reed. This was no easy feat. It was almost impossible to drive due to traffic. Frank would take the metro. That involved a train change from the blue line to the red line and then walking about one mile from the Red line to Walter Reed. Initially he walked through some tough neighborhoods and certainly he would not have walked through there after dark, but he witnessed the entire neighborhood change from essentially a dangerous area to an area that at first could be described as up and coming and later was a full-fledged cosmopolitan area with apartments, condos, shops and restaurants.

Frank was a supervisor in his capacity as a government civilian. He was in charge of a section of 14 military, civilian and contractor personnel. They were great employees and they had a great mission. Frank worked in distribution and it was his job to quickly and efficiently move equipment to supplies to both Iraq and Afghanistan (the other division moved the personnel although there was a lot of crossover). Anytime supplies did not have to be flown was a win as long as the required delivery date could be met. The sea lanes were essentially open so that commercial US flagged vessels could be used. The main issue was that containerized equipment would be offloaded moved by truck to bases in Iraq or Afghanistan then offloaded. The problem was that the units would use the containers for storage at the outlying bases. This was normal and was anticipated but not all contracts allowed for the quick purchase of containers that were used for storage. These were huge contracts that had to be negotiated over an extensive time period. This meant that Frank was often travelling to conferences to rewrite or modify the contracts. This caused Frank to cancel some of his Nephrology (Kidney) appointments. Frank was not very meticulous about rescheduling the nephrology appointments. The only thing that forced him to make an appointment was when he was almost out of prescription medicine. Frank's wife was in charge of him taking his medicine and ensured he would see the doctor in time to refill prescriptions prior to running out. Frank remained in denial that anything was wrong but he was the only one.

The bad thing about changing from a contractor to a government civilian was that Frank had to start over with his vacation. That was quickly rectified when almost as soon as he arrived there was a requirement to send a distribution expert to Iraq for an extensive (56 day) comprehensive study. The team had been put together for about one month but the Army staff did not have a logistics representative. Frank's boss asked him to send a military officer. He had a LTC that worked for him who was perfect for the job, but the LTC was finishing up a master's degree and the timing was bad. Frank told his boss that he would go and she saw no reason why a civilian could not go. Everyone agreed and Frank was told to make arrangements to leave at midnight the next night for Iraq with the rest of the team. Frank would also be able to supercharge his available leave days as these trips normally required everyone to work 7 days a week and that would qualify civilians for compensation time in the form of leave days. The late notification was actually and advantage. The other team members had to spend a week of classroom time preparing for the trip. They were also told they had to bring a classified laptop. That was a bad idea. No network administrator in their right mind would let a lap top hook up to a secure network anywhere at any time let alone in a combat zone. Frank took a regular laptop that could be connected to the NIRPRNET and that became the only usable computer for the team.

Even though Frank was the only civilian on the team he knew most of the other team members. The officer in charge of the team was a Colonel from the Joint Staff that Frank knew. The team was part of a large effort once again led by a three star general, but included intelligence, special operations, combat arms as well as logicians. Everything was being examined in theater. Most of the team members were told that they were hand selected because they were the best in their field. Frank certainly knew that there was a caveat that they were the best in the field who were reasonably available. But everyone thought that being on this team was a ticket to promotion. The team did consist of a lot of high caliber military men and women. Certainly the logistics team was well constructed. The Joint Staff, the Defense Logistics Agency, TRANSCOM and the Army Staff were represented. There were a few other members on the team that mostly provided admin support. The team spent the initial days in Kuwait. Since Frank had spent a lot of time in Kuwait he set up interviews at the various nodes throughout Kuwait. Frank quickly realized there were two types of organizations and leaders at the nodes. Some welcomed the team and quickly told them all of the problems they were experiencing and asked the team for assistance (which wasn't the role of the team). Other nodes and their leaders looked at the team as an interruption, tolerated their presence and basically told the team that they understood the mission they had been given and were perfectly able to accomplish the mission without the assistance of what one commander called men and women with notebooks. This was especially true of the Defense Reutilization and Marketing Office at Kuwait. The mission of the organization was to take all the excess that was being generated as well as things like scrap metal and see if other agencies could use the items or sell it. It was plain to see at a glance that his organization was well run. Instead of taking on the appearance of a junk yard, everything was laid out perfectly. Even the scrap metal was neatly arrayed thanks to a team of welders would cut the metal into manageable sizes and then stacked it up in the yard. The commander of the organization was a reservist who said he gets mobilized for every operation: Desert Storm, Bosnia, Haiti, Afghanistan and now Iraq. He knew how to run a yard. He gave us a command brief and while he was polite, he wanted nothing more than for us to leave so he could get back to work.

The team had a Navy Seabee assigned to it. On the Joint Staff, the engineers were in the J4 and were considered part of logistics. That was not the case at lower levels. Most engineers, to include Army, Marine Corps, Navy Seabees and even the Air Force Red Horse Teams, considered themselves operators. They could be used on a combat roles as well as a horizontal or vertical construction role. The team's Seabee showed up one day in full Battle Rattle. He announced to the Team that he had had all he could stand of being with loggies in Kuwait and he had talked his way into a helicopter ride to Al Basra and from there a riverine unit would take him up river. The Colonel objected, but we really were not doing much if any Engineer evaluation so he let him go. Frank began calling him COL Kurtz from Apocalypse Now and said he was going up river to form his own Army of Kurds. In any event, he was going to hitchhike through the combat zone and write his own report of the engineering situation in theater. We never heard from him again.

Frank set up a trip to Baghdad for four members of the team. A regularly scheduled logistics meeting was being held at Saddam's Palace and although it was tough to get an invite, Frank succeeded. They flew to Baghdad on a C-130 and attended the meeting. It was an eye opening experience. The theater had a very sophisticated method of tracking distribution. In fact, the entire logistics mission could be summed up in one word: distribution. Frank was proud to see that the training that was done years ago at Fort Bragg and other bases was being implemented. Convoys were now call Ground Assault Convoys. They were integrated into every aspect of the fight. Communications systems for convoys were improved and systems that were previously domain of the combat vehicles, were now being installed on convoy vehicles. Convoy commanders conducted rehearsals and some of the larger installations even set up rehearsal areas. The ability to call for fire and to call for medevac was validated. Redundant systems were set up in the event that a leader's vehicle was destroyed or disabled. Stock Status were displayed in real time or near real time. Water, fuel and, ammunition were pushed based on forecasted demands. Repair parts and replacement vehicles were intensely managed. While the mission was to ensure the forward bases had what they needed, there was a real attempt to avoid building the so called iron mountain that had been the norm in previous operations. All this was done under force structure caps and while trying to maximize the use of contractors. Most convoys had civilian trucks embedded in the convoy. All convoys included gun trucks, breach teams and the ability to call for reaction teams. Many convoys had to traverse numerous command areas and had to be ware at all time who could provide fire support, medevac and reaction forces in the event they were needed. This was occurring at the height of the insurgency and convoys were certainly a target, but the leaders in the theater worked hard to ensure that convoys were not a soft target and were in effect an extension of combat operations and fully integrated into operations. Since most convoys originated in Kuwait, the task was monumental. It was a great experience and a real honor to participate in the conference. The team went to fly back at the end of the conference and their plane had been rerouted on a higher priority mission. This was now like being stuck at a commercial airport. Missing your flight did not mean that you were automatically booked on the next flight as that was already full. The team hung around the terminal for a day and a half before they could get out.

When the team returned to Kuwait, they set up a trip to Bahrain and then a trip to Qatar. Frank was looking forward to the Bahrain trip as that would involve staying in a hotel. The Log team could have stayed in barracks in Kuwait and Frank and the Colonel probably could have scored a room but the rest of the team would be in an open bay and that would have been miserable. Soldiers in the open bay were on different schedules, would be awake at all hours of the night. It was loud, often reeked. Staying in the tents was far better.

Upon arrival in Bahrain, the hotel the team supposed to stay at was booked. The team had a fender bender at the airport that caused the team to miss the check in time. Frank contracted the Army Commander of the Bahrain Terminal and he hooked the team up with a hotel. He also took the team out for a night on the town. He was a Karaoke fan and took the team to a bar. He was so into karaoke that he brought his own guitar. Since Bahrain is often considered the Las Vegas of the Middle East the team had a great time. Frank was also able to go downtown, a first on his travels to the Mideast. He went by himself so he could get a break from the team (at this point they had been together for about 40 days). He went deep into the town and stopped at one of the many hookah bars. He sat down and at an outside table and had a bowl of apple wood tobacco lit next to him. He stayed there for about two hours and left totally relaxed. In fact he was so relaxed he hoped he would not be asked to provide a urinalysis sample when he returned to the Pentagon. As the team was wrapping up there was a shakeup at the highest level of the Defense Department. The SecDef and a lot of the staff were removed. This made the evaluations being conducted by the team became more important.

Frank took two more trips to Afghanistan. The first was a quick trip to attend a conference in Bahrain and then conduct a site visit in Afghanistan. The mission was to examine the viability of establishing alternate routes, that could take advantage of rail and ease some of the pressure on the Pakistan Ground Lines of Communication that either had to go through the Khyber Pass or the Chaman gate in the South. While these were subject to interdiction, theft, strikes and weather, at least they were exclusively civilian and did not involve US soldiers traveling through dangerous or hostile territory.

The team arrived around midnight and went to the dining facility for a midnight meal. Frank had a cold slice of pizza and a mountain dew. Other members of the team were convinceded to try a stew that the local Afghans had made. Having the pizza was the best decision Frank had ever made as the rest of the team became violently ill. Afghanistan is not a good place to get sick as the air around populated areas is not all that healthy to begin with. If you got sick, it was not very likely that you would recover and the team members other that Frank spent most of the time in the barracks. They did manage to go from Bagram to Mari A Sharif and reported that a Northern Distribution Network appeared to be viable. While this network involved numerous transloads, it did not rely on trucks until arrival in Afghanistan. While it was a greater distance the rail and ferries could travel 24 hours a day and once up and running provided a steady line of communication into the theater.

His last trip to Afghanistan came when Frank could tell his kidneys were failing and in fact they did 60 days after the trip. It was a great trip however. Colonels and GS 15s Frank's Government rating) were banned from going to Afghanistan, but Frank's job had changed to a pay for performance and he was in a pay band. No one knew what that was, so he and the program manager were allowed to travel. When they arrived in Afghanistan, they were treated like GS 15s which meant they received priority for flights. Frank and the program manager had their own fixed wing aircraft and could travel all over the country. Frank did know that travelling with his kidney issues was not the best idea but he did not want to pass up the trip. He was already suffering from cramps and dehydration and he had to wake up every 60 minutes to go to the bathroom (from the tent to the porta john). Waking up was not really an issue at Bagram Air Base as fighter jets were lifting off less than 200 meters from the tent all night long. Not only was it loud, but the pressure from the jet engines actually could be felt in your chest. He was worried that it would really embarrass his unit at the Pentagon if he had to get medevac'd out, but when he was in Afghanistan he saw people that were in their seventies, and people that were hundreds of pounds overweight. It seemed anyone available could be hired as a government or contract employee if they were willing to go to Afghanistan. It was a great trip that resulted in real changes being made to manage the almost exclusive use of commercial ground transportation in Afghanistan.

Epilogue

Most of this novel was written while connected to a dialysis machine. On 26 July 2011, he received a kidney transplant. The kidney was donated by his sister. His sister volunteered to do this and had to undergo numerous tests to ensure compatibility. These tests were done at Walter Reed Army Medical Center and since his sister had no affiliation with the Army, the Army Surgeon General had to approve this testing. She was found to be compatible, but there was a final glitch. Walter Reed was shutting down and transferring to Bethesda Naval Hospital due to the Base Realignment and Closure Act. Both his sister and Frank were told that they would have to wait until September until after the transition. This could have voided some of the tests. On July 1st they were told that there would be an opening for one last transplant on 26 July. The date was locked in; the operation was performed on that date and was a success.

Frank is no longer on dialysis. Frank wants to emphasize two points. You can have a decent life while on dialysis. The other thing he would like to emphasize is the sacrifice that his sister made. His sister had two college age children that participated in activities that his sister and brother in law attended. Their son played intercollegiate football and their daughter was studying abroad in Australia. His sister and her husband were looking forward to traveling and being part of their children's final years in college by attending games and education milestones. She took a huge risk to donate the kidney. That she willingly undertook this risk that could have jeopardized a well-deserved life of travel and adventure sport activities to include mountain climbing, skiing and back packing, speaks volumes about her character. She entered the operating room a strong, confident, mother, sister, daughter. In fact, she and her husband summited Mount Kilimanjaro in November of 2010. She had spent so much time at altitude that her red cell blood count was high and that almost disqualified her. Fortunately the doctors and nurses were used to dealing with Special Forces troops and soldiers who operated at altitude to include those serving in Afghanistan and were aware of the effects of altitude. The Doctors and Nurses at Walter Reed also were used to seeing highly athletic people but they were all impressed by her strength, courage and sense of humor.

The Doctors, Nurses and the staff at Walter Reed were simply amazing. More than technically competent, they were upbeat, positive and had a genuine concern for the mental wellbeing of the patient as well as the physical. They could not have been better, from the surgeon to the technicians. Frank was also impressed that everyone working in the hospital had a self-improvement plan. The Army medics had a plan to become clinical specialists, the nurses were taking courses in management or a specialty area, the doctors were constantly teaching or taking developmental assignments. Everyone had a goal and all were actively pursuing that goal.

The operation was a success and it has now been five years since the transplant occurred. His sister had truly given him a second chance at life. She has been able to return to hiking and skiing. She also has been very involved in assisting wounded warriors and their families participate in ski vacations in Colorado. The author lives in Fayetteville, North Carolina and volunteers for a nonprofit.

CPSIA information can be obtained
at www.ICGtesting.com
Printed in the USA
LVHW022311210319
611507LV00007B/176

9 781478 789826